SING ME A MOON

When Goda Makin sings down the moon for her son, Petroc, the boy believes he can achieve any ambition. But this is 18th century Cornwall and his first love, Catriona Bostock, is out of reach for a fisher boy. Growing from ambitious boy to vengeful man, Petroc Makin sets in motion a train of events which will affect many people. Most of all it will affect the lovely Tamar, whose own attempts to sing down the moon bring her into the gravest danger.

CATHERINE DARBY

SING ME A MOON

Complete and Unabridged

LINFORD
Leicester

First published in Great Britain in 1980 by
Robert Hale Limited
London

First Linford Edition
published 2000
by arrangement with
Robert Hale Limited
London

British Library CIP Data

Darby, Catherine, *1935 –*
    Sing me a moon.—Large print ed.—
    Linford romance library
    1. Love stories
    2. Large type books
    I. Title
    823.9'14 [F]

ISBN 0–7089–5727–7

Published by
F. A. Thorpe (Publishing)
Anstey, Leicestershire

Set by Words & Graphics Ltd.
Anstey, Leicestershire
Printed and bound in Great Britain by
T. J. International Ltd., Padstow, Cornwall

This book is printed on acid-free paper

Part One

1695

1

When Petroc was a small boy one of his greatest pleasures was to lie in his pallet when darkness had fallen and listen to his mother sing as she moved about in the kitchen below.

They called it the kitchen, but it was really the living-room with only a slip of a chamber at the side where his parents slept, and the railed edge halfway up the wall where his own pallet was laid. When he had climbed the ladder he could stretch out and peer sideways through the bars into the dimly lighted apartment below, and watch his parents as they sat by the fire or cleared away the day's untidiness before they retired to their own bed. The kitchen was virtually the whole house, its white-washed walls darkened with soot from the wide hearth where all the cooking was done, its stone floor covered by rush matting that was rough and warm to bare feet on a cold winter morning. Apart from the scrubbed pine table and two high-backed cushioned chairs there were only a couple of stools, a cupboard and an ironbound chest in the whole place. His mother kept linen and clothes in the chest and her dishes and jars in the cupboard. Her pans and ladles and the big carving knife were ranged along the walls, and from the railed ledge dangled bunches of onions, and hams smoking in the fragrance of rushlight and sea coal, and bundles of thyme, sorrel, lavender and parsley with which she flavoured food, mixed poultices, and sweetened her underwear. Above the hearth hung the gleaming sword and scabbard that Petroc's father had worn during the Civil War, when he had been a very young officer in Cromwell's army.

'My brother, Elias, was killed in that war,' was all that he would say when his small son pressed for details of the campaign, and his pleasant face looked

4

so tight and angry that Petroc never asked any more questions.

There were many things he would have liked to know about his father. Luther Makin was not a Cornishman though he had lived in the west for nearly forty years, and he was neither a farmer nor a fisherman though he wrested a living from both soil and sea.

All that Petroc knew was that he had left his native Yorkshire and come penniless into Cornwall. The farm on which they lived had been left to him by a young man called Robert Masters who had died in the same war that carried off his brother Elias. Of his family in Yorkshire or of the life he had once led there he never spoke. Only when he looked at the sword did a bitterness tighten his mouth and cast a shadow over his eyes.

Petroc knew far more about his mother, who was Penzance born and bred with cousins and half-cousins and uncles and aunts scattered thick as fleas between Helston and Land's End.

'The Penhallows never made any money but they surely knew how to breed!' she would exclaim, half joking but with a sadness in her voice, for after twenty years of marriage she had only one living child, though six small head-stones below St Michael's Church bore the names of four other boys and two girls who had preceded him.

Petroc wondered sometimes what those other babies had been like and if his mother had sung to them as she sang to him.

'I loved your mother before I even saw her,' Luther Makin said.

'Tell me about it,' Petroc urged. He'd heard the tale many times before and never grew weary of the telling.

'I lived here alone on the farm at the time,' Luther would relate, and there were days when I felt like turning my back on it all and venturing to foreign lands, but I'm not one to be beaten, so I stayed here, fighting to make sufficient profit to live. On this particular day — '

'It was November,' Petroc said.

'Aye, it was November,' Luther agreed. 'I'd walked over to the headland to get a breath of air for it was damp, mizzling weather with no breath of wind. I was low in spirits that day and I sat down on a rock and watched the gulls winging out over the grey water.'

'And heard the singing?'

'Clear and high and sweet as a bell, ringing across the turf and the silvery sand. I forgot all my troubles then. I sat and listened to the singing.'

'You thought it was a fairy woman, didn't you?'

'I did indeed and loved her directly, though up to that time I'd scoffed at such fancies. But I sat there, listening to that voice and feeling all my troubles melt away, and I loved the one who sang.'

'And then she walked out on the beach below you.'

'Gathering kelp from the rocks.' Luther nodded. 'She had on a brown cloak and green hood, and I was still half-convinced she was a fairy!'

But fairy women did not limp, Petroc knew. They were never born with one leg shorter than the other so that they must wear a thick soled boot and sit with the old women when the young people danced. It was that deformity which had prevented Goda Penhallow from finding a husband though she was fair-faced with the voice of an angel. But men in Cornwall looked askance on women who had been overlooked by the piskies.

'I wed her a month later,' said Luther. 'It was the most sensible action I ever took in my entire life, for she has been the best wife a man could hope to have.'

He always ended up by smiling across Petroc's head at his wife who invariably blushed scarlet and told him not to be a great fool, and at such times the love between the three of them stretched tight as a cord of silver thread.

They had very few friends, partly because Goda was too conscious of her limp to enjoy going into company, and partly because, for all that he had lived so long in the district, Luther Makin was still regarded as a bit of a foreigner. The farm he had inherited from his wartime comrade was no more than scrubland on which crops grew grudgingly, when they grew at all, and Goda's dowry had long since been swallowed up in a new roof for the barn where the cow and two horses were stabled, and in a little boat that Luther rowed out beyond the shallows on the days he went fishing.

'Good lobsters and crabs fetch a pretty price at market.' Luther said, 'and there's nothing like a smoked herring to put flesh on a man!'

That was a regular joke too, for both he and Petroc were thin and rangy with long legs and light hair that flopped over their temples. Goda declared that in their winter cloaks they looked like grasshoppers bundled up in hay.

But when the fishing was done, and the lessons learned, and the cow milked the best part of the day remained. Full of oatcakes and ale and juicy crab, Petroc would submit to a hot flannel rubbed over his face and a stiff brush to smooth the tangles from his hair and then it was up the narrow ladder to the railed platform where he would lie like God looking down on his own private world, and listening, as the rushlights flared low, to his mother's singing.

She sang in the old tongue but needed no words, for the notes soared beyond speech into a region where there was only beauty. And when the year drew to its close she sang of winter so sweetly that Luther declared the birds delayed their migration in order to listen.

But the best times Petroc decided, were when he had been sick, or had cut his knee climbing up the sharp rocks to the headland, or when the lobster pots had been empty or rain had washed away the new planted seedlings. At those times Goda would take off her apron, unbind her long hair, and sit with folded hands in her chair, her face raised to the unshuttered window.

'Be still now,' she would command. 'Be still and I will sing you a moon.'

And her voice, soulless as the wind, would rise up to the square of sky beyond the window, weaving an intricate melody in which every note both stood alone as something perfect and complete and, at the same time, echoed and enriched all its fellows.

Petroc never understood how it happened, but whenever his mother sang the moon whatever had been wrong no longer seemed very important. His cut knee stung less sharply, his tooth ached less unbearably, the lobsters would be back the next morning fighting to get into the pots, and the rain would enrich the soil so that the next seedlings planted would yield more profitable harvest.

And always, when she had offered the last drifting note to the silent sky, the moon would rise beyond the window and seem to hover for a moment.

'To bed now, my love,' she would say, unclasping her hands and binding up her hair.

Petroc would climb the ladder and pull the coarse woven blankets around his shoulders and fall asleep to the sound of the wind beyond the house and the low voices of his parents as they tidied away the dishes and shuttered the moonlit window.

Those were the times that meant most to him, for he was still at the age when each day had a colour and a flavour of its own, and it was hard to remember the previous week. He had no idea what it meant to be bored, for his life was full of tasks to be performed from the milking of the cow and the feeding of the hens to the sowing and reaping and the bringing home of the catch from the lobster pots.

'The boy must be educated,' Goda said. 'He must learn how to read and write and figure, so that he may get on in the world.'

'Education never did me much good,'

Luther said, but he made no further objection and, for part of each day, Petroc was set to the forming of pothooks and the adding of figures.

Lessons came easily to him and he had read all his mother's small store of books before he was ten. Goda herself read well and wrote a pretty hand.

'For when I was young I could not run with the other children, so my father declared that I should be taught book learning as well as sewing and cooking,' she explained. 'There are great adventures in books and 'tis wondrous strange to read them.' But life itself was an adventure, Petroc thought. They lived so isolated that even a chance meeting with a neighbour was something to be remarked and discussed over the supper table.

That was until he saw Catriona Bostock for the first time and knew he didn't want to talk about it to anyone.

He had been familiar with Bostock Towers for as long as he could remember. The great turreted building dominated the windswept headland above the bay, and Sir Taverne Bostock was a well-known figure in local parts.

'A rich man,' Luther said, a faint wistfulness in his tone as if he contemplated some discarded ambition of his own. 'He owns much of the land hereabouts, not to mention properties in Devon. His father acquired a small fortune during the Protectorate and the son has added to it.'

'He dotes upon his daughter,' Goda added. 'Her birth cost her mother's life and Sir Taverne has never taken another wife.'

Petroc had never paid much attention to talk of the daughter. Sir Taverne he had glimpsed once or twice, pink-coated on a black horse, with hounds snapping about. The great house had reared its bulk against the skyline throughout Petroc's life. High walls topped with sharp glass surrounded the ground and the iron gates were kept locked save on rare occasions when a closed carriage bowled through them.

It was rumoured that from time to time Sir Taverne went on a drinking spree with two or three boon companions, and that on such occasions his young daughter was sent from home until her father was his own man again. Petroc paid little attention to such scraps of gossip as filtered back to him and, having no wish to have his ears cropped for trespass, had never ventured near the house.

On this particular morning he was, however, feeling unusually restless. Part of it had to do with its being spring, when the rising sap seemed to course through his own veins. Part of it had to do with his own dawning consciousnes of himself as no longer a child but a youth who would soon be fifteen. His wrists and ankles shot out of the breeches and shirts that Goda mended so carefully, and he often woke shivering from delightful but disturbing dreams. Luther was over at Helston, a list of provisions in his sleeve for at this time of year Goda always declared she had run out of every household necessity. Goda herself was cleaning the house from top to bottom, laying the linen under large flat stones in the brook where she could beat it to her heart's content before hanging it dripping over the hedgerow. Her normally smooth brow was puckered and her voice had an unaccustomed edge to it.

'For the Lord's sake, Petroc, take yourself out somewhere. You're under my feet!'

He could have gone into Helston with his father, but Luther had already left, and the prospect of a long day confined to haggling over prices ill-matched the boy's mood.

Instead, grabbing his jacket before that too disappeared into the stream with the rest of the laundry, he headed for the beach. At this hour he usually had the expanse of seaweed covered rocks and fine sand to himself, and for a while he could run and jump and fling sticks and use up some of the

16

energy that burst out of him in such moods.

It was a disappointment therefore when he reached the bay to see hoofprints marked along the sand and to hear the furious barking of a dog.

In another moment or two the animal bounded towards him, its feathery tail wagging furiously, its coat already tarnished with damp sand.

'Hey, boy! Hey, dog!' Petroc dropped to his knee, snapping his fingers. The dog ran up, sniffing cautiously and then licking with every appearance of delight. Across the sand a high voice called imperiously, 'Belle! Heel, Belle!'

A slim, black-haired girl on a white pony cantered up and drew rein, staring down at him as he knelt.

'He's a friendly pup,' he said approvingly.

'Belle is female!' There was scorn in the girl's voice. 'Cannot you tell the difference?'

'Dogs ought to be male and cats

female,' Petroc said, 'to match their natures.'

'What a strange idea!' the girl exclaimed. 'Do you have many such?'

'I reckon not, leastways none I could voice,' he said awkwardly, squinting up at her from under his lashes.

Her riding habit was deep red and her hair fell in shining coils from beneath a small feathered hat. He was aware of narrow dark eyes and a small mouth and lowered his own gaze to the dog again.

'Belle's a pretty name,' he said.

'It's French for 'beautiful'. Do you know any French?'

He shook his head. 'I know some Cornish,' he volunteered.

'Peasants' talk!' Again her scorn tinkled out and the pearl handle of her whip gleamed as she moved her hand. 'My father will not have the old tongue spoken in his presence. He says we must look forward into the future, not cling to the outworn traditions of the past.'

18

'My own father says the past shapes the future,' Petroc argued.

'Who is your father?' she enquired.

'Luther Makin.' He hesitated and then enquired in turn, though he had already guessed the answer. 'Who is your father?'

'Sir Taverne Bostock. How silly of you not to know that!'

'I've heard of him.' Petroc rose laconically and began to brush down his sand-spattered breeches with the edge of his hand.

'He's the most important man in this neighbourhood,' she said indignantly.

'So they say.' He leaned to stroke the dog again.

'I am Catriona Bostock,' she announced.

'I told you cats ought to be female!' he exclaimed, and blushed uneasy lest he had presumed too far.

To his relief her laughter rippled out more naturally with no affection of scorn.

'And do you have a name. boy?'

'Petroc Makin, mistress.' Recalling his manners he attempted a bow and slipped on the wet sand.

'Good morrow to you, Petroc Makin.' She gave a small tight smile, lips closed over her teeth.

'I've not seen you before,' he said, marvelling a little at the way the world changed from day to day. Staring at her he was conscious of horizons receding.

'You will know me when you see me again,' she said, and her own cheeks were pink.

'You never ride out along the beach.' he objected.

'Because it is forbidden. My father cherishes my safety.'

'But you are here today.'

'Because it is forbidden.' she said and laughed again, opening her mouth to show white, sharp teeth.

'And will you ride here again?' he asked.

'I might.' Her dark lashes fluttered. 'Then again I might not. It depends on how I feel.'

'I might come,' he said, matching her casual tone. 'I might come if the mood is upon me, but I have work to do.'

'What kind of work?' she asked.

'This and that.' He spread his hands. 'I help my father with the lobster pots and on the farm and I have lessons to learn.'

'Lessons?' Her black brows arched.

'Used to have lessons,' he amended. 'I am near fifteen now and past learning.'

'I had a governess,' Catriona said. 'She was from Paris.'

'Was?'

'She fell down some steps and hurt her back,' the girl said. 'After that she was often sick and cross, so my father sent her home. That was a year ago and I've had no governess since.'

'And live at Bostock Towers.' He gestured towards the cliffs.

'Much of the time.' She moved her shoulders restlessly. 'I stay with friends often.'

Petroc wondered if she knew about her father's drinking bouts. Something in her expression warned him to be discreet.

'It must be a goodly life,' he said at last. 'Visiting other places, meeting people.'

'It suffices,' she said briefly.

There was a little pause, interrupted only by the dog's whining as she jumped up for attention.

'I'll come again,' Catriona said suddenly. 'I cannot tell you when it will be, but I will come again.'

'When it is forbidden?' Never having felt under any compulsion to rebel, he asked the question with some surprise.

'Especially when it is forbidden,' she returned serenely. 'Hand Belle up to me if you please. I ought to go back to the house now. My father is away but the servants sometimes chatter.'

He handed up the dog, his fingers brushing her gloved ones. For an instant her narrow eyes sparkled at him, and then she wheeled around in a flurry of sand and galloped off, without looking round.

'Catriona Bostock,' Petroc said. The name had a strange, subtle flavour in his mouth. With the toe of his boot he traced her initials in the sand and promptly scuffed them out with his heel. He'd had a fancy to hunt for gulls' eggs, but now all desire for such pastimes had deserted him. Yet the restlessness was still inside him.

'They were saying in town today that taxes are to be raised again.' Luther told his wife and son as they ate supper later that day.

'Are we not sufficiently taxed?' Goda asked. 'It seems to me we pay more and more into the government coffers!'

'Rumour whispers we'll be paying more.' Luther scowled into his ale.

'I'd like to see anyone try to collect more taxes,' Goda said. 'The last man was thoroughly ducked in a cesspool before he was ridden out of town.'

'Sir Taverne Bostock has undertaken

to send agents in, or so the talk goes.'

'Always talk,' Goda shrugged. 'Petroc, what are you gaping at?'

'You mistake a gape for a yawn,' Luther said. 'Are you tired, lad?'

'Middling.' Petroc closed his mouth firmly and sat up straight.

'What have you been doing with yourself all day?' Goda enquired.

'Nothing very much.' He shrugged and pushed his bowl away.

'I chased him out from under,' Goda said. 'No doubt he's been wasting time.'

'Youth's the age for that,' Luther said tolerantly.

'You'd best get to bed now,' Goda said. 'If there are more taxes to be found then we'll need to work harder for profits. Be up with you now.'

Bending to kiss her cheek he noticed a patch of white at her temple. It had never struck him before that his mother was growing old, but he was conscious of the white hair and the lines on her neck. And his father was beginning to stoop. He had never noticed that before either.

'Goodnight, love.' Goda twisted her head to look at him and her eyes mirrored the awareness in his. 'We'll need to put a brick on your head soon,' she commented. 'Why, you're growing fast into a man!'

In that moment he had the perverse notion that it was better to be a child again, his father erect, his mother's hair brown. But the world had moved on since the morning. He had met Catriona Bostock and given up hunting for gulls' eggs.

As he stretched out on the pallet and looked down into the kitchen Petroc heard his mother say, with a catch in her voice that might have been a sob or a laugh, 'We'd do well when the taxes are paid to try to put by a little for the future. The day will come when the boy will have need of it for his own younglings.'

But that was far ahead, Petroc thought, rolling over and pulling the covers up to his ears. As he drifted into sleep he left behind the sound of his mother's voice and ran, in dream, across shifting sand to a girl in red on a white pony.

2

'The boy is in love,' Goda said thoughtfully.

'Our Petroc? He's a child!' Luther exclaimed.

'Children are capable of much loving,' Goda informed him, 'and Petroc is growing up into manhood very swiftly. He will be taller than you are, my dear.'

'And in love already?' Luther looked amused.

'He had all the signs of it,' Goda informed him. 'Forever combing his hair and going off into a daydream whenever he is required to do any work!'

'And who is the object of our son's affections?' Luther enquired.

'That I cannot tell,' Goda admitted. 'I wondered if you could — '

'Ask him? I'll do nothing of the sort,'

Luther said. 'If the lad's old enough to be in love he's old enough to keep his secret to himself. You'll have to restrain your curiosity.'

'I want him to be as happy as we have been,' Goda said.

'Petroc is barely fifteen. Don't condemn him to matrimony before his time,' Luther grinned.

'Condemn indeed!' Goda glared displeasure and then laughed. 'I hope he has found a girl who will keep him in order. If he resembles you she'll have her hands full!'

'I hope he's found one with a handsome dowry,' Luther said. 'After this wet summer I dread to think what the harvest will be like. The grain is well-nigh drowned already.'

'Will we be able to get through the winter?' Goda looked anxious.

'We've plenty of supplies laid down,' Luther assured her, 'but the land is due to be re-rated and even in a bad harvest there's always the chance they'll increase my tax.'

'You pay four shillings in the pound now. They cannot value this place at more,' Goda protested.

'Unfortunately they can, and once the rate is fixed it's the devil's own task to get it altered.'

'You could refuse to pay.'

'And in my youth I may have relished the fight,' Luther said, 'but I'm sixty-seven years' old, my love. That's too old for conflict.'

'If our other children had lived — ' Goda began.

'We'd have had more mouths to feed.' Luther reached across and patted his wife's arm. 'We'll make out,' he reassured her. 'Sir Taverne's not sent out his agents yet, so there's every chance he's on one of his drinking bouts and may not get round to it.'

In that opinion he was mistaken, Sir Taverne Bostock was, at that moment, at the handsome desk in his equally handsome study, a ledger in front of him and an untasted goblet of brandy at his elbow. His eyes were thoughtful and his voice sharp as he addressed the man seated opposite.

'Three times this past fortnight, you say. And how often before that?'

'I cannot say. I didn't know until recently that Mistress Catriona was in the habit of slipping off alone.'

'It's your business to know! I pay you sufficient for the purpose.' Sir Taverne said irritably.

'I cannot be everywhere.' the man said sullenly. 'The young mistress does not take kindly to being followed.'

'And I don't take kindly to having my daughter run in company with a yokel! What do we know of the Makins?'

'Not much, sir, for they keep themselves to themselves. The father is a Northern man. There's talk of his having been a gentleman once.'

'Which means he's a bad farmer now.'

'The farm is small, sir, but prosperous enough though the soil is hard to work. Makin ekes out a living with his lobster pots.'

30

'Is he a drinking man?'

The steward shook his head.

'Women?'

'No, sir. He's been happily wed for years. The woman's a Penhallow, piskie-touched in the foot.'

'I've seen her. Fair-faced with a thick soled boot.'

'She's a quiet body, seldom leaves the house. The boy is her only son.'

'About fifteen, you say?'

'Looks older. A lusty lad,' the steward said.

'He'd best not lust in my daughter's direction,' Sir Taverne snorted.

'You want something done about all this?'

The steward's tone was somewhat lacking in respect. Sensitive to it Sir Taverne said coldly, 'I'll attend to the matter myself. You'll keep quiet about it. My daughter will not become the subject of gossip.'

'Very good, sir.' The man rose and bowed, eyes lowered.

A sly fellow, Sir Taverne frowned,

when he had left the room. But useful. Exceedingly useful when information was required.

He reached for his brandy and swallowed a couple of mouthfuls. The liquid warmed his throat but his mind remained cool. Only on those occasions when he set out to drink his companions under the table did he allow himself to become fuddled. But he had no desire to imbibe too deeply when there was a problem to be solved. Sooner or later he had known the question of Catriona's future would arise, but he had fallen into the habit of regarding her still as a child. Now he walked across the room and stood, hands behind his back, gazing up at the portrait that hung on the panelled wall.

He had loved his beautiful, high-spirited wife passionately and her death in childbed had taken all the gaiety out of his life. He had never looked at his daughter without a flash of bitter grief, and when the grief became too much to endure he sent Catriona to his cousin's estate and settled down to drink himself into oblivion.

The dark eyes of the woman in the portrait reproached him with neglect of his parental duties.

'I'll arrange her betrothal,' he said aloud. 'She's of an age to be settled with a man of good family. I'll not have her run wild over the countryside with a peasant whose father is not even a Cornishman. I'll see she is reared into the society of her class.'

The eyes reproached him still. He swung away and picked up his brandy, draining it at a gulp. Then he sat down again, drawing towards him a pile of account books. It might be as well to check on the Makin property, especially with the rates due to be increased.

'I will have to go back soon,' Catriona said, lazily stretching. 'My father is at home, closeted with his steward, Dawes. Creeping Dawes. I always call him, for in truth I cannot abide the horrid man!'

'He has not insulted you?' Petroc

asked, sitting up abruptly.

'Only by his continued existence,' she said. 'He's a tiresome creature, and I am certain he is employed to spy upon me.'

'I should like to catch him following me!' Petroc exclaimed, clenching his fist.

'It makes no matter. I shall probably be going away on a visit again soon.'

Her voice was so casual that for a moment the words had no meaning for him. Then, as their import struck him, he stared at her in dismay.

'Going away on a visit! Where?'

'To one or other of my cousins, I suppose. You did not imagine that I would rusticate here for ever, did you?'

'When will you leave?' he asked miserably.

'Soon, I expect.' She shrugged elegantly. 'My father has stayed sober for three whole months. The time is approaching when I will be packed off before his drinking companions arrive.'

'And what of me?' Selfish in his

disappointment, he spoke petulantly.

'You will be gathering in the harvest, helping your father with the fishing.'

'It will be poor exchange for your company,' he said.

'A poor harvest too, after so much rain. They say the peasants will go hungry.'

She spoke idly, having little interest in the plight of peasants.

'Must you go away? Surely you have the right to stay at home if you wish.'

'In that great pile of stone?' She nodded towards the cliffs, her mouth drawn tight. 'It has fifty rooms and nothing in any of them to amuse me. You would not condemn me to a winter there, would you?'

He shook his head, hoping that it was not simply a desire for amusement that led her to seek his company. For his own part the day was bleak that did not contain a sight of her.

She sat now on a flat, turf-cushioned stone, her back supported against the sloping cliff, her legs stretched out in front of her. His eyes followed the long line of her thigh beneath the olive green habit. She had taken off her hat and her black ringlets spiralled from a centre parting. At her throat an opal flashed fire from a handsome golden brooch.

'I wish you would not stare at me so,' she said abruptly.

'I like to look at beautiful things,' he said simply.

She blushed and dimpled but said, still peevishly, 'I am not a thing but a person.'

'Yes, of course.' He lowered his eyes to the buckled boots that showed beneath the hem of her skirt.

In his mind Catriona Bostock was not a girl like the girls he occasionally saw in Helston. Those girls could be teased and joked with, but Catriona's face and figure were like those glimpsed in a dream. For Petroc her reality was bounded by the beach where she rode her horse and the tamarisk fringed slopes that reached to the edges of the spray drenched rocks. In the months they had been meeting he had never kissed her, and the only times they touched was when she set her hand on his shoulder to remount her horse.

'And I have the right to enjoy the society of other people,' she continued.

'Yes,' he lied, knowing that were it within his power he would keep her always with him alone.

'After all, you are not the most amusing person in the world,' Catriona said, as if she were determined to be provoking. 'There are times when you are exceedingly dull.'

'Then I'll leave you to the amusement of your dog,' he said angrily, springing to his feet.

Belle, as if aware that she had been brought into the conversation, looked up, thumping her tail.

'Help me to mount.' She too had risen and stood with averted head as he whistled the pony to him.

The light pressure of her hand on his shoulder and a glimpse of white stockinged ankle as her foot groped for the stirrup dried his mouth and brought a pounding to his temples. He stooped and handed up the little dog.

'I will come again,' Catriona said abruptly, 'and, if I do visit my cousins, I'll stay for only a short while.'

Her dark eyes were kinder than he had known they could be. He had an insane hope that she might bend and kiss him, but she only smiled with closed lips and cantered away again across the sand.

A path curved up below the cliffs to a gate in the walls of the grounds surrounding her home. She rode it fearlessly, though the rain had made it treacherous in parts. There were times when she wished she could go on riding for ever, beyond the horizon, without having to dismount and enter the great, echoing house where portraits of her mother gazed down in every room.

'Is that you, Catriona?' Her father emerged into the side hall as she came in.

'Who else would it be?' she asked,

offering her cheek for his kiss. 'Nobody ever comes here.'

'Are you reproaching me, my dear?' He drew back a little and smiled down at her in a faintly rueful manner. 'Indeed you have cause, for this is a dismal house when there is no company present. I have been thinking of taking you on a long visit. Would you enjoy that?'

'Are your friends coming?' she asked.

'No!' he answered sharply, the artless question pricking his conscience. 'No, with a long hard winter coming up I have decided that it would be an excellent idea if we were to close up the house and travel for several months.'

'Together?' she enquired in surprise.

'Why not?' Looking at her he stifled the familiar stirring grief. 'You're a young lady now, my dear, and ought to see a little of the world before you are wed.'

'Wed!' She stepped back a pace. 'I'm not old enough to be wed.'

'But you're old enough to meet

young gentlemen of good family. I'd not wed you off to a stranger, nor to a man for whom you had no fancy.'

His eyes, as dark as her own, raked her face, but she stared back with no sign of discomposure. Evidently, her friendship with the Makin boy had made no very deep impression upon her.

'If the Court were gayer. I would present you there,' he said heartily, 'but William is a dull dog. Never mind, my dear daughter, we will make shift to entertain you while we travel together!'

He wished she would confide in him, but perhaps Dawes had been exaggerating and there was nothing to confide at all. He sighed inwardly, wishing she were less like her mother. To be constantly in her presence, without recourse to brandy, would be a sacrifice for him. He would be glad when she was comfortably married and he no longer had to smile as if her resemblance to her mother pleased him instead of tearing his heart.

'Catriona Makin,' Petroc said in a low voice.

He wanted to yell out the name but there was always the chance that somebody might hear. He could not have endured questions or ridicule.

'Catriona Makin,' he said again, and ran across the beach to the stony track that ran between high banks of couch grass towards the farm.

It had never occurred to him before how small the house looked, its roof low, its doors and windows crouched under the eaves.

He bent his head beneath the lintel and paused for a moment, his glance sweeping the long, low-ceilinged room. It smelt, as usual, of spices and herbs and the unmistakable odour of lobster. His mother was darning, a pile of woollen socks spread out on the table. Her head was bent, her hand moving in rhythm as the needle wove in and out.

'You're blocking the light,' she

complained mildly. 'Either come in or go out again, my dear.'

'Where is father?' he asked, coming further into the room.

'He went out an hour since to see if he could catch something for supper. Did you not see him?'

'I was over in the bay.' He dropped to his stool and reached for a hunk of bread.

'He went from the north shore. I told him it was too late in the day but it's never any use trying to talk sense into a man when he's an idea in his head. That bread is fresh-baked, so watch your fingers!'

'It's good!' he said.

'There'll be little enough of it in months to come if we don't get a week's sunshine to dry out the harvest,' Goda said.

'We have supplies laid down.' He gave her his father's argument.

'And will have to sell some of those if the land tax is increased overmuch,' she returned gloomily.

'It's not like you to have the dismals!' he rallied.

'My head is troubled with a heaviness in it,' she said. 'There'll be a storm later.'

'The sea is calm as a millpond!'

'There are banks of cloud rolling in from the west. By midnight the storm will be upon us.'

It was certainly growing darker. After a few moments Goda bundled the darning up into the basket and rubbed her eyes.

'You'd best walk up to the gate and see if your father's on his way,' she said. 'He'll need to beach the boat high tonight.'

Petroc went out again into the stillness. It was not yet the turn of the tide but a dull, green light permeated the landscape and not a bird sang. A couple of heavy rainfalls would flatten the harvest. The rye and barley were already dark with moisture, the stalks bending under the weight of water.

At the gate he stopped, watching a

figure ride towards him. The man sat a plump pony and wore the Bostock livery under a heavy cloak.

'Master Makin? Be your father home?'

The man was one of the grooms. Petroc knew him by sight, though he had never had occasion to speak to him.

'He's out fishing,' Petroc said.

'Sir Taverne is getting out the rate demands in good time for Christmas!' the servant told him.

'Rate demand? We've had no agent around.' He took the sealed document and frowned at it.

'Likely your place isn't worth the checking. Will you see your father gets that? I was to hand it to him direct, but I'd like to get back before the rain starts.'

'I'll see to it.' Petroc nodded as pleasantly as he could, reminding himself that the man was simply doing his job.

The letter in his hand he started back

towards the house and paused. The seal was not firm. By inserting a fingernail between it and the paper he could unroll the document and roll it up again without anyone being the wiser.

He hesitated a second longer and then unrolled the paper and stared down at the black inked words that ended in the flourish of Sir Taverne's signature.

'Eight shilling in the pound!' he exclaimed aloud, the words on the paper leaping up in the fading light. There must surely have been some terrible mistake. The farm had been valued at a thousand pounds which meant they would have to find four hundred pounds before the spring. It was seldom that the profits even touched ninety. This demand was either a mistake or an attempt was being made to drive them from the land. He stuffed the offending demand inside his jerkin, and went on through the gate.

Mist was deadening all sound, blanketing the hedges and dropping a curtain over the moors beyond.

He began, without noticing, to run towards the shore, his feet slipping on the rutted lane. But sea and sky had merged into a uniform greyness. Tendrils of fog reached out like fingers to clutch the land. He shivered, aware of the damp creeping through wool and leather, to lay seize to his bones.

His father would be becalmed in such a sea. He would have to rest oars until the fog lifted and the sharp needles of rock that menaced the shallows were visible again. It had happened before and there was no sense in getting alarmed.

A rent of strange brilliant light tore the sky apart, and spray drenched his face and hands. Petroc had a glimpse of water boiling up into whirlpools and then the fog rolled in again. From beyond the headland echoed the dull rumble of approaching thunder.

Petroc went slowly back, walking with caution, his eyes piercing the mist. Another crash shook the landscape and the leaden sky glowed molten copper.

'Is there any sign of your father?' Goda called from the doorway.

She had lit the rushlights and in their glow, a shawl over her head, she looked old and vulnerable.

'He's not back yet.'

'It's so dark,' she said anxiously, 'and the wind is rising. The sea can be so treacherous.'

'He'll be safe. Father's been fishing these parts for years,' Petroc comforted.

'But he wasn't born to it, just as he wasn't really born to farming. He was born a gentleman,' Goda said.

'Up in Yorkshire. Yes, you told me.'

'He could have been a rich man,' she persisted. 'He might have travelled the world but for my sake he stayed in this little corner of it. He sacrificed much for me.'

'He'll come to no harm.' Petroc said.

'I've put more bread in to bake.' She shrugged as if she were ridding herself of a burden and went back inside.

'I'll bring in some more logs,' said

Petroc. 'We'll build the fire up, ready for his coming.'

'I think I'd like you to walk back to the shore,' Goda said. 'It would be a help to set flares, lest he's near enough to see them.'

'If you like.' He stooped for flints and tapers. 'Have I time for a mug of cider?'

'I'll pour it for you.' She limped to the table and poured it, foaming and brown, from the stone crock.

'You're not usually so anxious about him.' Petroc drank deeply.

'I feel a weight on me,' she said. 'I've felt it all day, like a band of steel ringing me round, pressing down on me. It's the storm, I expect.'

'Listen to that wind!' he exclaimed, setting down the mug and opening the door again. It tugged at his fingers as if the wood had a life of its own, and the shutters rattled violently on their hinges.

'It'll be worse down at the shore,' Goda said. 'He'll have to ride the shallows until morning.'

'The gale will blow out the torches,' Petroc said. 'There's no sense in trying to light them.'

'I'll go down to the shore myself,' Goda said. 'Luther will need help to beach the boat.'

'He'll never even try to approach land,' Petroc said. 'He'll ride out the storm. We'd show more sense in waiting.'

It was useless, he knew, to suggest that she might go to bed while he waited up. Already she was settling herself by the fire, a rug over her knees. Silently he closed the door against another gale of wind and shot the heavy bolt into its socket.

'You ought to sing a moon,' he said rallyingly, kneeling to pile more wood on the hearth.

'This is no night for singing,' she said gravely. 'The wind roars too loud and I've an emptiness at my heart.'

'I ought to have gone with him in the boat,' he said guiltily.

'Then I'd have been left to wait

alone,' she said. 'On this night I'm grateful for company, my dear.'

His thoughts had sped to Catriona. On the heights the lightning would crack around Bostock Towers, reflecting itself in the many windows. He wondered if she were abed in some shuttered, silk-hung chamber, or if she sat alone, listening to the fury of the elements.

But thinking of Sir Taverne's daughter at this moment was a kind of betrayal. Catriona was safe and warm, while somewhere beyond the treacherous rocks his father was tossed in a narrow boat.

'He'll be home at dawn,' he said loudly. 'He will be home, won't he?'

His mother made no answer, but he heard her sigh as another growl of thunder threatened the fog-bound eaves. And then the wind blew more violently.

3

'It would have been easier for me to bear if we had found his body,' Goda said. 'A man ought to have a grave, not be sucked down under the sea.'

It was, of course, possible that the body might still be washed up in some bay or port, but so far only pieces of the boat had been found, snapped off and already barnacle encrusted, with only the red letters of the name to prove it had been Luther's vessel at all.

'Ladymoon,' Petroc said. 'Why did he call it that?'

'It was the name of the house where he was born,' Goda said. 'A big house on the moors below York, he told me. He quarrelled with his father when he was little more than a boy and came south.'

'And called the boat after his old home.'

Petroc, who had never considered the matter before, grew thoughtful. 'Has he any relatives living there still?' he enquired.

'He never spoke of any, and I never asked.' Goda gave her son a sharp look. 'If it's in your mind to seek help from that quarter you may forget it,' she warned. 'He never was beholden to them in his lifetime, and I'll not go against his wishes now that he's dead. We'll manage this place together, my dear, and accept charity from none.'

She spoke proudly, with the confidence of ignorance. The matter of paying rates had slipped her mind, and Petroc had not yet told her about the increase. It nagged at his own mind, however, like an aching tooth that no clove could relieve. By early spring four hundred pounds had to be found, and it was certain that the ruined harvest would yield no profit at all. The grain was beaten down by the gales and sodden with the heavy rain. Neither, until he acquired another boat, would it be possible to go fishing.

He wondered if any of his mother's relatives might help. Since the night of the great storm there had been a constant stream of Penhallows, all come to condone with their kinswoman, but their patched boots and shabby clothes spoke of a poverty greater than his own.

There remained the possibility of appeal to Sir Taverne Bostock, and that appeal would have to be made swiftly for rumour had it that Bostock Towers was to be shut up for the winter while Sir Taverne and his daughter were away.

It was one thing to decide to appeal to Sir Taverne, and quite another to put it into practice. Petroc had never been within the gates of the mansion in his life, but he supposed that a man on legitimate business would be admitted.

'I'm riding into Helston,' he informed Goda in reply to her questioning look at his boots and cloak. 'Is there anything I can bring back for you?'

To his relief she shook her head, smiling a little. He guessed that she imagined him to have put on his Sunday clothes because he was going to court a girl. She had hinted pretty strongly once or twice that his Penhallow cousins were growing into comely women, and he knew she would be glad to see him settled.

'Take care of yourself,' he said unexpectedly.

'I reckon I can make shift for a day,' she returned impatiently.

He nodded, hoping that his absence would only be for a day. Sir Taverne might, after all, be induced to be reasonable.

The rains had eased, but fallen trees and fences bore witness to the havoc that the recent storms had caused along the coast. He rode slowly away from the low, white-washed house, turning only once in the saddle to wave to his mother. In the month since his father's death she had aged visibly, her hands shaking a little, her eyes, that were still a pretty shade of blue, red-rimmed from the tears she would not shed in front of Petroc.

Beyond the small farm lay the moors with the ribbon of road winding towards Helston. Petroc made his way at a leisurely trot away from the main track towards the headland. The path was narrower and steeper here with loose shale to impede the way. Sir Taverne had never bothered to improve the road that led towards Bostock Towers, probably because he wished to discourage uninvited guests. As a landowner he was a very private man, as a justice of the peace he was harsh but fair. So ran his reputation in the district.

The wrought iron gates were locked as usual. As a small boy he had stood hand-in-hand with his father and gazed up at those gates.

'A rich man lives there,' Luther had said. 'When I was young I too hoped for riches, but I've learned sense since then.'

The memory of that long ago afternoon rushed over the boy, and his eyes pricked with tears. He had not really grieved for his father until this moment, and at this moment he had no time for grief.

'Were you wanting something?'

A voice, rusty with age, from a shrub at the other side of the gates, made him jump. The owner of the voice hobbled into view and peered at him through the bars.

'I have business with Sir Taverne Bostock,' Petroc said.

'Nobody said anything to me,' the old man grumbled.

'It's urgent business, granddad. You're to open up quickly.'

'I'm opening up, I'm opening up.' The gatekeeper jangled a bunch of keys. 'And I'm nobody's granddad either. No conniving female ever put a ring through my nose!'

'Good for you,' Petroc approved, riding through the reluctantly opened gate.

'You'd do well to follow my advice,' the old man said. 'The house is ahead of you. Tradesmen to the back door.'

He had already locked up again and was shambling away.

The avenue stretched upward between sloping lawns dotted with clumps of bush and trees twisted by the wind into a variety of weird shapes. The drive ended in a handsome courtyard round which the four-storey building rose in forbidding fashion. There was neither grace nor beauty in the edifice, but it had a certain grandeur.

He dismounted, swallowed hard, and tugged at the bell rope outside the door. There was a moment's pause and then the door was pulled inward, as slowly and reluctantly as the gate had been.

'Yes?' The servant had a lofty, superior air in keeping with his surroundings.

'Master Makin on urgent business with Sir Taverne Bostock.'

'Are you expected?' The servant looked faintly surprised.

'He will see me,' Petroc said, hoping

he sounded more confident than he felt.

'You'd better wait inside then.' The door opened a fraction wider.

Petroc tethered the horse to the post at the side and followed the man into the high vaulted chamber with a fireplace at each end and a twin staircase descending from a gallery above. Light slanted dimly from high, narrow windows and brilliant rugs hung against the walls and splashed colour over the flagstones.

'You're to come this way,' the servant said, returning.

Petroc swallowed again and followed the man through a side door and down a short corridor into a panelled apartment with leather chairs and couches and velvet drapes. There were glass fronted shelves lining every wall, and not an inch of space between the handsomely bound volumes. Goda, who was so proud of the half-dozen books she possessed, would have been in a seventh heaven here.

'So it's the living son and not the dead father who comes calling without an invitation,' an amused voice said.

A tall figure had risen from the shadow of a deep chair and was surveying him from hooded eyes. It was possible to trace dimly in the proud features a resemblance to Catriona's young loveliness, but Sir Taverne's face was lined, his voice hard.

'I am Petroc Makin, sir.' The boy bowed, hat in hand.

'And well grown for your years. I was sorry to hear about your father.'

'It was a great loss, sir,' Petroc said sombrely.

'Your mother took it bravely, I've no doubt? Women have a way of dealing with grief that mere men cannot follow.'

'She was hard hit, sir, but she's not one to show her feelings.'

'And now you wish to see me. You've a good reason for disturbing me, I hope?'

'It concerns the rates,' Petroc said.

'I had a notion it might,' Sir Taverne

said dryly. 'Few seek me out for the pleasure of my conversation, I find.'

'Your servant brought the tax demand, sir, on the day my father went out in the boat and never came back.'

'A coincidence I regret.'

'My father never saw the demand, sir, and I've not yet shown it to my mother.'

'So you take it upon yourself to open letters, do you?'

'I do what I feel is right,' Petroc said.

'And pave your own road to hell, I've no doubt.' Sir Taverne regarded him frowningly and said abruptly, 'And did you take it upon yourself to bring the money too?'

'Four hundred pounds is too much,' Petroc said. 'Our farm is scarcely worth ninety a year, and since we lost the boat — '

'You want more time in which to pay? I cannot make exceptions to the rule.'

'But you already did.' Petroc interrupted. 'You set our rates too high.

Four hundred pounds is not a fair estimate.'

'So you are a valuer of land, are you?' Sir Taverne sat down at the flat-topped desk and nodded amicably. 'You set yourself high, young Makin!'

'Not as high as you would set my property!' the boy flashed. 'Even if I had such a sum I'd not pay it on principle.'

'A farmer with principles! You interest me more and more.'

'My father was a gentleman,' Petroc said levelly. 'He and my mother taught me to read and write and reckon.'

'You father was a stranger to me,' Sir Taverne said coldly. 'I've no interest in his accomplishments or his station. I'm not entirely my own master in this, you know. Certain sums of money must be raised in every district so that the government can offset some of the cost of the Irish campaign.'

'We cannot afford it,' Petroc said.

'How true! But King William does not ask for my advice or your opinion,'

Sir Taverne informed him. 'I have a certain figure to raise and you, in common with everyone else have no option but to pay.'

'And if we cannot pay?' He asked the question boldly.

'If you or anyone else cannot pay, you can always appeal in the courts for a reduction.'

'It costs money to go to law.'

'You're intelligent,' the older man approved. 'If you cannot pay you could cut your losses. The farm would be forfeit, but your mother has relatives who would take her in, I suppose.'

'Her kinsfolk are very poor. They couldn't help,' Petroc said, 'and the farm is my mother's home. She's lived on it all through her married life. She's too old to put down roots anywhere else. If you cannot remit the tax nor give us time, sir, there is another suggestion I have to make.'

'I'm listening,' Sir Taverne said, 'though I cannot imagine why. If I'd any sense I'd have thrown you out the instant you stated your business.'

'You could pay the rates on the farm yourself,' Petroc said.

'Out of charity?'

'Sometimes a man may borrow against a mortgage.'

'You do have some education, don't you!' Sir Taverne exclaimed in sarcastic pleasure. 'So I'm to hold the mortgage on your farm, am I? It's worth nothing to me, and if you cannot afford your tax, how do you expect to keep up repayments on the loan?'

'There is one other way,' Petroc said. 'I could leave the farm, sir, and make my own way in the world. There are ships sailing from Falmouth and riches to be gained in other lands. If you took a chance on me, sir, I'd come back in a year or two and pay all that I owed in tax, with interest as well.'

'Leaving a run-down farm and a lame widow as security, I suppose?'

Sir Taverne leaned back, watching the bright, angry colour flush the boy's face, noting the clenched hands that denoted anger held in check. The lad was no peasant, that was certain. There was breeding in that face and a determination in the set of the shoulders.

'You're sure this isn't an excuse to run off and make a fortune for yourself?' he demanded.

'I would come back and pay the debt. You have my word on it,' Petroc said.

'If you come back you'll pay more than the debt,' Sir Taverne said. 'There are fortunes waiting to be made, young man, for those who are strong and not afraid of a little danger. Prize money to be picked up if you've a mind to tangle with pirates on the Spanish Main. Gold in the Americas, if you don't die of fever or get shot to death by blowpipes. You might return as rich as Midas!'

'But without the asses' ears, sir!' Petroc said.

'Wit as well as the impertinence of the devil!' Sir Taverne chuckled, the sound an unfamiliar one in his own ears. 'I've a mind to take a chance on you, Petroc Makin. I was a great gambling man in my youth, and it seems to me that I've little here to lose. How did you propose setting out on this quest for riches?'

'By signing on a ship.'

The boy's voice betrayed a slight uncertainty.

'Leaving your mother to think you as dead as your father, I suppose?'

'I intended to write to her, sir, to let her know I was safe. There'd be no sense in waiting for her permission, for she'd not give it.'

'There's a ship — a trading vessel called the Lady Mary — docked at Falmouth,' Sir Taverne said. He had drawn a sheet of paper towards him and was writing busily as he talked. 'Captain Ferguson is a friend of mine. A hard man but a fair one, and his crew respect him. He sails for the Mediterranean tomorrow. I'll give you a letter for him. A reference. If you don't live up to him, don't come whining to me. It's usual to sign on for five years, but Captain Ferguson might make an exception in your case. That'll leave you free in a year or so to return home or travel further afield without having to jump ship.'

'That's very good of you, sir,' Petroc said.

'You haven't heard my conditions yet,' Sir Taverne said briskly. 'Your basic pay will run to about twenty pounds a year, but there will be prize money from salvage and a share of the profits from any trading venture. A prudent man could retire wealthy.'

'You said there were conditions,' Petroc reminded him.

'In return for my paying the rates on your farm, you will give me a half share of any profits you make over and above your wages.'

'That's fifty per cent!' Petroc exclaimed.

'To be paid into the bank at Falmouth under my name. Captain Ferguson will arrange bills of exchange for you. He knows how these matters are arranged.'

'And my mother?'

'I'll go and see her myself,' Sir Taverne said. 'I'll tell her that on my advice you have decided to venture into a wider world than the farm.'

'But the farm will need to be worked. And the lobster pots are undamaged.'

'You want me to hire labour for the place too? Very well, I'll undertake to do that as well.'

'Then I thank you, sir.' The boy spoke politely but stiffly.

He resented having this final choice thrust upon him, Sir Taverne knew. But a youth with such promise of strong character ought to be thrust out into the world, not tied to plough and lobster pots. And there was Catriona.

'We plan to close down this house and travel,' he said. 'You were fortunate that we had not already left.'

'I would have followed you,' the boy said calmly.

'Lord! I believe you would!' Sir

Taverne exclaimed. 'But you have not told me if you accept my conditions.'

'I accept them,' Petroc said.

He had not offered to sign any agreement. Sir Taverne noted with amusement. Presumably he expected his word alone to be taken. The older man decided to take him at his own valuation. It was, after all, little enough to do for the lad.

'Gentlemen usually drink to an agreement,' he said, rising and pouring two measures of brandy.

'To our agreement, sir.' Petroc raised the goblet and drank, choking a little as the fiery liquid hit the back of his throat.

'Stronger than cider, isn't it? You'll learn how to drink rum before you're much older.' Sir Taverne put down his own goblet and began to seal the letter.

'Captain Ferguson of the Lady Mary. I'll remember that, sir.'

'You rode here, I take it?'

'Yes, sir, and brought a change of clothing.'

'Ready for instant travel. I like a man who is prepared well in advance,' Sir Taverne said. 'There'll be no time for farewells if you mean to reach Falmouth before the Lady Mary sails.'

'But you will go to see my mother? She will fret otherwise.'

'She will fret anyway,' Sir Taverne said, 'but I'll quieten her fears. Here's the letter, boy. Half of any profits you make is the bargain between us.'

'If anything did happen to me — fever or blowpipes — '

'I'd not turn your mother out. You've my word on that. Good luck to you, Master Makin.'

Sir Taverne dismissed him with a brief wave of the hand as if he were tired of the interview, and sank again into the deep chair.

Petroc took a last look at the crowded bookshelves and the portrait that was exactly like Catriona and went out. He liked Sir Taverne no better than before, but he respected him, and the prospect of becoming rich was an enticing one, though half of it would have to go into Bostock coffers.

The great hall was empty and echoing, with no servant to escort him to the main door, and it was cold despite the bright burning of the two fires. He stood in the middle of the apartment and looked round, savouring the richness of wood and carpets. This was the most splendid house he had ever been in, and the white-washed farmhouse dwindled even more rapidly in his mind.

'Petroc?' The sound of his name, echoing in the deserted hall, made his scalp prickle.

'Mistress Catriona.' He bowed, sensing that within her own domain she would expect formality.

'What are you doing here?' she demanded.

'I had business with your father.'

'I heard about your father.' Her voice had softened a little and she descended lower, pausing to look down at him, with her hand resting lightly on the curving balustrade. 'I was truly sorry.'

But she had not ridden down to the farm to say that she was sorry. She had never displayed the faintest interest in his parents or in the place where he lived, and his coming to her home had violated some unwritten rule between them.

'I am going away,' he told her. 'I am going to sail to the Mediterranean, probably further.'

'But who will take care of the farm?' she asked.

'That has all been arranged. As a gentleman's son I don't intend being a farmer all my life.'

'So you're going to make your fortune?'

There was amusement in her voice, and a hint of patronage that grated on his nerves. He stared up at her silently, imprinting her image on his mind.

A rushlight in a wall sconce behind her outlined her head in a soft glow. Her black ringlets were bunched at each side of her head, each coil twined with thin red ribbons. Her gown of silvery grey had matching ribbons threaded down the full sleeves and round the stiffly frilled skirt.

'I may be away for a long time,' he said in a rush. 'I may be away for years, but I will come back. I'll come back and make you my wife. I give you my word on that.'

He filled his mind with one last, hungry glance at her, and then, not waiting for a reply, turned and marched briskly to the door, his head held high as if he already contemplated the vastness of oceans.

The girl on the stairs opened her mouth as if she meant to call him back. Then she shrugged and went slowly back up the staircase, her head drooping a little.

The door into the corridor closed quietly and Sir Taverne went back to his library. He was not angry at what he had just overheard, for it had merely confirmed his opinion that the Makin boy had character. It was to be hoped that he stayed away until Catriona was safely wed to a man of her own rank.

Even as he decided that he sighed. The boy might well become rich, and his manners would gain polish when he had travelled a little. As a son-in-law he might have proved an interesting companion, but no! Catriona would have aimed much higher for her beautiful daughter.

He returned to his chair, shifting it around so that he could look directly at the portrait. His wife had been descended from Spanish grandees and her dark eyes and hair would have graced the finest palace in Castille. She had died before her time, and left him with nothing to fill his life. There was only Catriona to love, only Catriona for whom to make plans. And those plans could not be allowed to include an impertinent young man called Petroc Makin, whose father had been a gentleman, but who had neither rank nor fortune to recommend him.

Part Two

1710

Part Two

1710

4

The August sun turned the water to gold and sent patterns of light winging across the sand. Above the bay the cliffs were yellow with gorse and inshore the seaweed had a patina of brightness.

Petroc raised his face to the loveliness, screwing up his eyes against the glare. It was surely a good omen that he had come home on such a fine day. For an instant as he glanced towards the high walls of Bostock Towers he wondered if a miracle might happen and Catriona ride down the winding path with Belle perched on the saddle before her. But that was foolish. Belle would almost certainly be dead by now and it was unlikely that Catriona came down to the beach these days. But some fragment of boyhood dream still clung to him.

The bay, despite its loveliness, was

deserted. He had ridden here straight from Falmouth, gold from his last trip weighing down his saddle bags, his cocked hat at a rakish angle.

He could have easily stayed overnight in the bustling port. The girls passing by eyed the tall, sun-burned stranger with open invitation. Against his tanned skin his sunbleached hair looked almost white; his grey eyes had darkened to blue. There was a casual elegance in the set of his blue coat and fall of lace at cuffs and throat.

'Will you settle down and take a wife now?' John Frazer had asked.

Frazer was ten years older than Petroc and occasionally talked as if his friend was no more than a schoolboy. They had explored many places together, shared danger and the occasional woman, argued and laughed and drank in a hundred different ports, but it was understood between them that their ways would part when Petroc left the sea.

'I've been shinning up masts since I

was nine years old,' Frazer had said. 'I'd have no place on land.'

'I'll go home first,' Petroc said.

'And settle to farming again?' Frazer raised an indulgent eyebrow.

'And settle to courting my bride, if she'll have me.' He laughed as he spoke, for it seemed inconceivable to him that she could possibly refuse.

In the years since they had met he had never seen a dark-haired woman without feeling a tug at the heart, and his greatest pleasure had lain in the memory of her as she stood on the wide staircase in the echoing hall of Bostock Towers. That she had never written to him meant nothing, for he had never written himself. Over the years there had been two or three brief, stilted missives from Goda. They had caught up with him long after they had been written and told him nothing save that his mother was well and apparently under the impression that he had run away merely to seek his fortune. He had written back, describing the beauty of

79

some of the places he had seen. He had not mentioned the hardships of a salt pork diet, of days made hell by constant seasickness, or nights when it was so cold that his fingers froze to the wheel and the breakers threatened to swamp the craft as it ploughed through the furrows of an angry sea.

Petroc had stayed relentlessly at his task, learning from his mistakes, saving the half of his prize money that he had agreed to keep, sending the rest to Falmouth for Sir Taverne. He had received no acknowledgement from Catriona's father, and had expected none just as he had never expected any letter from Catriona herself. In order to be accepted into their world he would need to prove that he was something more than a boastful boy. And he had, he thought, succeeded. Since Captain Ferguson's death he had sailed on two other ships, earning his Master's licence, working long and hard, gaining a reputation as a hard, close-fisted but honest man.

'I wish you luck,' Frazer had said. 'My thanks for your friendship.'

He had clapped Petroc on the back and turned on his heel, leaving the younger man with the horse he had just acquired. From now on they would return to their separate lives, and not seek to continue that friendship.

Now he stood alone on the sand, the reins of his horse looped over his arm. To the left Bostock Towers reared up into the blue sky, to the right the soaring cliff cut off his view of farmland and moor.

He remounted, humming under his breath, and rode slowly across the sand into the narrow gorge that cut a swathe between the rocks and led him up to the fields above. It had evidently been a fine summer for the crops stood tall, abundant in their glory of gold and green. He savoured the sight as he approached the house, his heart lifting as he took in the trim perfection of white-washed walls and a barn that had obviously been extended since his time. The farm looked more prosperous than he had known it.

In the yard he dismounted and raised his voice in a shout.

'Mother! Mother, are you there?'

The door of the house opened and a thin woman with fading blonde hair emerged, a child clinging to her skirt, a younger babe in her arms.

'My husband is at market, sir,' she said. 'I expect him at any time now if you're minded to wait.'

'To wait?' He dismounted slowly, looking at her in puzzlement. 'Where is Mistress Makin?'

'Makin, sir? Do you mean Goda Penhallow that was?'

'I mean my mother,' he said impatiently.

'Bless me, sir, but you must be Petroc Makin then.' Her dull face had lightened into realisation.

'And come home at last,' he said, wondering if she were slow-witted for she continued to stare at him.

'You went away to sea, long years ago,' she said.

'And now am home,' he repeated. 'Can you tell me where my mother is?'

'Mistress Makin died,' the woman said. 'About three years back she died.'

'Died?' He stared at her in his turn, trying to rearrange his thoughts. 'Are you telling me my mother is dead?'

'Three years back,' she nodded. 'She was old, you know.'

'Old? I suppose she was,' he said slowly.

'Past seventy,' she agreed.

'So she must have been.' He was silent for a moment, remembering with a pang how he had once noticed the grey in her hair. Odd that he had forgotten that until this moment. For him time had stood still.

'I'm sorry, sir,' she said. ' 'Tis a hard homecoming, I know.'

'It was to be expected, I suppose. Children don't realise their parents grow old. What happened, Mistress — ?'

'Mistress Dawes,' she said and bobbed a curtsy.

'Dawes.' The name sounded familiar but he couldn't recall where he had heard it. 'Are you lodging here then?'

'The farm belongs to my husband, sir,' the woman said. 'We've lived here these past five years.'

'Five — but you said my mother died three years ago.'

'But not here,' she said. 'She went on the parish after the farm came to us. I heard she died over at her cousin's place, the other side of Helston. I'm sorry but I don't know where she's buried, sir.'

'Dawes. Your husband worked for Sir Taverne Bostock, didn't he?'

'He was steward, sir, but he had a fancy for his own place, and this suited him. We've built two extra rooms at the back and put a new roof on the stables.'

'While my mother went on the parish!' The words forced themselves between his clenched teeth. At his temple a pulse beat rapidly.

'I'm sorry, sir,' she said nervously, 'but if you'd like to step in and wait for my husband, he can tell you about it better than I can.'

'I'll not wait,' he said curtly, and swung himself to the saddle again.

His grief at the news of his mother's death had blazed into a furious anger. So Sir Taverne had foreclosed upon the mortgage and broken his word! It would be the last time he revoked a promise, Petroc decided grimly, as he rode towards Bostock Towers.

His fury had hardened to an icy ferocity by the time he had reached the gate of the estate. Leaning from his horse he tugged at the bell, shouting at the same time in a voice hoarse with rage.

'Open these damned gates, blast you!'

A young man in shirt and breeches ran down the drive and fumbled with the bolts. Either he was new to the position or Petroc's expression frightened him, for he swung the gates back and touched his forelock without enquiring the visitor's business.

The great house had not changed. He dismounted and stared up at the gaunt facade, its windows veiled against the sun. The door, however, stood open, perhaps to provide warmth though, as he stepped into the hall, he was plunged into chill.

This apartment too had not changed. Bowls of dried grasses decorated the empty hearths, and the rugs were a little more faded, but the atmosphere of dignity remained.

There was a rustling along the gallery, and he looked up to see Catriona descending the staircase. He had the sense of having been whirled back into time, to being again the boy who watched the lovely young girl on the staircase.

She paused near the foot of the stairs and he saw that the girl was a woman now, the promise of beauty fulfilled. Certainly she was richly gowned, as if she were proud of her appearance and wished to provide a fitting background for it. Her dress was a blend of scarlet, orange and gold, fire colours that blazed about her dark dignity. Her black hair was drawn up over a frame of gold wire and ribbons of gold lace were twined around her long ringlets. Under the elaborate headdress her face was pale and composed, the lips tinted scarlet, the eyelids brushed with blue.

'Mistress Catriona.' He found it hard to speak over the lump that had formed in his throat.

'You have the advantage of me, Master — ?' She tilted her head slightly, her voice enquiring.

'Surely you have not forgotten me?' he said.

'Is it — Petroc Makin? Are you — but we assumed you had gone for good — dead even!' She was stammering, her hand twisting the brocade of her dress.

'Very much alive,' he said grimly. Now that he had absorbed the full impact of her appearance his anger was rising again.

'I assumed you dead,' she said again.

'But surely your father told you that money was being paid by me into his bank account at Falmouth.'

'My father died six years ago,' she said flatly. 'I take no interest in his financial affairs.'

'And my mother is also dead.' His eyes accused her. 'Dead these three years. Did you take any interest in that?'

'My husband administers the estate,' she said. 'The affairs of the tenants and neighbours are not my concern.'

'Husband?' The word stabbed at him. 'I told you that you were going to be my wife!'

'Told me, but you never asked!' she snapped.

'It was understood between us. We needed no words.'

'Don't shout, or the servants may hear,' she begged.

'You expect me to bow politely and wish you good fortune?'

'You'd best come upstairs,' she said, turning abruptly on her heel. Following her, Petroc was filled with a confusion of emotion. Rage and disappointment struggled for mastery, and underlying them was the desire to hold Catriona close and push away the intervening years.

She led the way into a room that opened off the upper gallery and turned again to face him, her expression wary. The room itself was lit by gleams of sunlight that slanted through the narrow windows. He had an impression of cushioned and curtained luxury. Then his gaze returned to the woman who stood before him.

'You were my choice,' he said. 'You must have known it. I went away to make myself worthy of you, to earn money and prove myself a man of honour. I gave you my word I would return.'

'Fifteen years later!' She burst into mocking laughter. 'It's fifteen years since you said those words to me! Dear

God, but you can't be in your right mind if you came back expecting me to be still waiting for you!'

'How long have you been wed?' he demanded.

'Eight years,' she said. 'I married my cousin, Jeremy Bostock, eight years ago.'

'One of your own class?' he mocked in his turn. 'Did you love him?'

'Love? I'm not a peasant, to live my life through another!' she said scornfully. 'We agree well together, Jeremy and I.'

'So well that he leaves you alone here, to answer the door to visitors?'

'He's in London until the end of the week,' she said.

'And leaves you here?'

'You left me for fifteen years,' she returned. 'I don't think you have the right to talk ill of him, or any other I might have chosen to wed.'

'Then let's talk of other things,' he said, moving closer and looking down at her. 'Let's talk of the bargain your

90

father and I struck. He told you about that, I'm sure.'

'And if he did?'

'You should have honoured his commitments after he died. It was a moral obligation.'

'Don't preach morality to me,' she said sharply.

'When my father died my husband took over all the estate and its affairs. If he chose to turn your mother off and give the farm to Dawes, that's his concern.'

'You're no faint-hearted child,' he accused. 'Had you wished you could have prevented it, but you didn't did you? You did nothing but sit in your fine house clad in your fine garments, while my mother was put on the parish and died, and all the time the money was being paid into your father's bank, money that comes now to your husband and yourself! You knew full well that I was still alive. You knew it, Catriona, and you greeted me with a lie on your lips!'

91

'After fifteen years you were fortunate to get any sort of greeting,' she returned.

'And I am to thank you for the honour you have shown by receiving me at all. I suppose? You were ever a proud wench,' he said.

'With reason,' she said. 'My mother was of high Spanish stock, my father a member of one of the oldest, most distinguished families in Cornwall. We have rank and breeding and wealth. How could you think to match that?'

'With love,' he said sadly. 'My parents loved each other at sight and I believed it was like that for us too. Oh, I knew that I would not be allowed to pay court to you until I had proved myself. I knew that even then your father would never look upon me with favour. But together we might have persuaded him, you and I.'

'You take too much for granted,' she said sulkily. 'I never thought of you in such a way.'

'And how do you think of me now?' he demanded.

'I don't have any opinion,' she said stiffly. 'You have grown and prospered, and it seems you have some right to be angry if nobody informed you of my father's death.'

'When my mother was turned off the land,' he interrupted, 'the bargain ceased to be. Yet for five years half my money has been paid into your estate.'

'You could go to law,' she said, 'but your case is weak. This 'bargain' was never written down, was it?'

'It was a verbal agreement made between gentlemen of honour!'

'Then go to law and sue for the return of your money. It makes no difference to us, for we can well afford to pay, if the Court so orders,' she said, 'but the case might drag on for years, and we are so highly respected in these parts I doubt if you'd find a lawyer to act for you.'

'You've grown hard,' Petroc said, and thought, even as he spoke, that he was mistaken. She had not grown hard but had always been so. Only her youthful beauty and his romantic illusions had blinded him. The most terrible part of it was that, knowing her nature, he desired her still, not with the tenderness of affection but with the cold lust of sensuality that seeks to destroy whatever it embraces.

'I wish you would stop staring!' she exclaimed suddenly. 'I cannot abide being stared at.'

'Shall I touch you then?' He stepped close, encircling her throat with his hands, smiling into her dark eyes. 'I never used to touch you, did I, save to help you to and from your horse? Do you like it better when I touch you?'

'My husband — '

'Is in London until the end of this week. You told me so yourself. There are no servants within call, else you'd have screamed for them the moment I laid hands upon you.'

'Jeremy will kill you,' she said in a small, choked voice.

'Jeremy will never know,' he returned. 'If a man leaves his woman unguarded that woman would be a fool to admit that an intruder had scaled the wall!'

'You'd not dare!' she panted. 'No gentleman would — '

'I am not a gentleman. You rightly reminded me that I am not in your class of society.'

'I order you to release me!'

'I am neither your horse nor your dog,' he returned. 'And you are not echoing with your eyes the words your lips speak. You tell me to leave and your eyes beg me to stay.'

'You lie!'

'No, I speak the truth and keep my word. I said I would marry you and I'll do that, in flesh if not in fact!'

She began to struggle, her nails raking at his cheek, her feet kicking out at his shins. Energy flowed into him and with it all the strength of his disillusionment. And all the time her eyes invited him.

'I loved you,' he heard himself moan

amid the rending of silk and the scattering of hair ribbons. 'I loved you well but you betrayed me, and lied, and cheated. For that you'll pay, my lovely wench!'

She had ceased to struggle and lay limply beneath him, her eyes half-closed, her ringlets damp with sweat. He took her over and over again, squandering his anger and his lust, and she made no sound. Only her body quivered beneath him and long sighs shook her as her hands clasped him to her.

'Say something to me,' he said at last, easing himself away from her.

Her eyes opened fully, blazing at him as, raising her head, she spat at him.

He rose tiredly, pulling up his breeches, wiping his face with the edge of his cuff. His hands were shaking and he craved the relief of tears. When he was ready he paused, looking down at her as she lay, despite her tangled hair and her torn garments she still retained an air of cold dignity that defeated any triumph he might have felt.

'Goodbye, Catriona Bostock,' he said.

There was nothing to add. He was bidding farewell to the girl who had ridden to meet him on the beach, to all the dreams he had treasured for fifteen years, to the boy he had once been and would never be again.

He walked along the gallery and down the wide staircase into the high, echoing hall. The door still stood open and the place was apparently deserted. In fifteen years the grandeur and the loneliness had not abated.

Something had ended on this day and could never be regained. His mother was dead, the farm lost, his love sullied. The sun mocked him as he remounted his horse, burning down upon his fair head. He had endured tropical suns with hope in his heart, but now hope was gone and Cornwall was a cruel place.

Riding down the avenue between the oaks he longed to be away again, to build a new life in a spot where he had neither hoped nor felt the absence of hope. It would be possible to sign on again, as Master of his own vessel this time. But he was tired of the sea and of life aboard ship. He wanted to sink roots deeply into the earth, to build something lasting that would endure.

Catriona was not for him even though he had taken her. With the same ruthlessness that had brought him back to claim his love he now drove that love from his mind and heart. Never again he swore silently, would he be caught in the toils of love. He would marry a healthy woman who would be obedient and upon whom he could beget children. And never would any of his children be forced to prove they were worthy of a love that was worthless.

He had no desire to go back to the farm, or to seek out any of his Penhallow relatives to enquire how his mother had died or where she was buried. It mattered little. Goda was dead and would never again sing down a moon.

'Ladymoon Manor,' he said aloud, and wondered how the thought had leapt into his mind.

Ladymoon Manor was the house where his father had been born and reared. Luther Makin had broken with his family and left Yorkshire, but he had called his fishing boat 'Ladymoon'. It was possible that a Makin still owned the place. A cousin with a handsome dowry perhaps?

The last of his boyhood was withering in the heat of the sun. As the groom hurried to open the gate Petroc took one last look over his shoulder at the towering bulk that menaced the skyline beyond the trees. Bostock Towers was a symbol of his most ardent hope and most cruel humiliation. At Ladymoon Manor there had to be something better.

5

He was unprepared for the beauty of the moors. They stretched around him in wave after wave of purple and gold, and the air had a fragrance so sweet that it lingered like some half-forgotten melody in the recess of his mind.

He had travelled slowly through the August days, staying at small inns along the way, keeping to the main roads that reached up into the north. The dust was thick and white, churned up by his horse's hooves, and no rain fell. A little would be welcome, he reflected, noting that the short grass was burnt as yellow as the gorse, and that the rivers ran low.

The landlord at Otley had been a newcomer to the district and knew nothing of the Makins.

'Though I know the manor house, sir. A fine old building that dates back nigh on two hundred years. I can draw a route for you.'

He might have shied away from giving information to a stranger, but this one was evidently prosperous and gentlemanly, not likely to have robbery or murder in mind.

Petroc consulted the drawing now. The river marked on it was obviously the one that wound its sluggish course on his right hand. To his left the ground sloped upward to a high hedge, tangled with sweet briar and bramble.

He dismounted, securing the horse's reins to the branch of a tree. There was a grove of trees here, willow, elm and ash leaning together and half concealing the broken arches and crumbling pillars of what had evidently once been a large building.

'There was a convent down by the river once, sir,' the landlord had said. 'It was pulled down and stones from it used to build the manor, they say. But that was long ago.'

So long ago that now only arches and broken bits of wall reared up amid the trees, and weeds grew waist high where the nuns had once walked with downcast eyes and quiet hands clasped over rosaries.

The manor house must lie beyond the hedge. He strode up the grassy path and came at once to a gate hanging drunkenly on its hinges. At the other side yellowed grass spiked the air and beyond the neglected garden stood the house.

It was a long, low, many gabled building, its windows shuttered. There was a quality of endurance about it that appealed to him. 'Come rain, come wind,' it seemed to say, 'but I will be here when those who quarrelled and loved and ate and slept beneath my roof are gone.'

As he walked through the undisciplined grass the front door opened and a woman emerged. She stood for a moment, shielding her eyes from the sun, and then she came towards him, her voice high and excited.

'James! I've been waiting such a long

time that I began to fear you would never come!'

Reaching him, she stared up into his face and then her welcoming hands fell to her sides again.

'You are not James,' she said. 'You are not James at all!'

'No, mistress.' He spoke gently for she was very old. Her hair was coiled in a white plait around her head and her fingers were like twigs.

'No, you couldn't possibly be he,' she agreed. 'James was much older than I am, and I shall be eighty soon. I think it likely he's dead by now, don't you?'

'Very likely,' he nodded.

'Yet one can never tell,' she said. 'He was always a cunning devil, going away for long years and then returning. But if you're not James, then who are you?'

'Petroc Makin,' he said and wondered whether to bow.

'Makin? Petroc Makin?' She frowned and spoke irritably. 'There's never been a Petroc in the family. My father was a Joshua and my mother's name was Yoni.

There was Aunt Hepzibah too and my sisters, Hope and Mercy. My brothers were called Elisha and Luther. Not a Petroc among them.

'I am Luther Makin's son,' he told her.

'Luther's son?' She peered at him in astonishment. 'Luther begot a child then. He ran off to Cornwall or some such place, you know. Quarrelled with my father and broke with us all. I forget the ins and outs of the matter. It was so long ago when we were young. How is Luther?'

'My father died when I was a boy,' he said, still speaking gently, he had no desire to cause her grief. She was evidently too old for strong feelings however, for she merely raised an eyebrow and said calmly,

'I'm surprised he ever settled down and lived long enough to raise a boy. But come into the house, do! No sense in standing out here for ever!'

The main door led into a small entrance hall with three doors leading off it. The door on the left was open, displaying an enormous apartment that was obviously both kitchen and dining-room. The old woman turned to the right and led him into a handsomely panelled parlour.

'Sit down and I'll pour you some wine,' she said hospitably. 'I don't drink much myself, but it's pleasant to have company for once.'

He sat down in the high backed chair she indicated and looked about him. The floor was carpeted, the hearth swept clean and decorated with dried grasses. It reminded him briefly of the summer hearths at Bostock Towers, but he shut out the memory and concentrated instead on the few pieces of carved furniture, the long tapestry curtains. Everything in the room was clean and neat.

'I keep the whole house in readiness,' she said, following his glance, 'lest James comes back.'

'Not by yourself surely!'

'Much of it. I'm stronger than I look,

young man! But little Emma Rowe comes over to help me clean. Her grandfather Eben was steward here long ago, and his wife Jessie was maid. They had many children but most of them are gone now, dead or moved away. The eldest of them was named Eben for his father. He married a girl from Harrogate and they've two sons apart from Emma. Lazy lads! I chase them away if ever I see them near, but Emma's a good child.'

He was not much interested in the Rowes. What did fascinate him was the skinny little woman who now perched opposite him. Despite her age her eyes were bright and her voice youthful. Her dress was sadly out of date, ruffled with lace and spangled with little flowers as if she were going to some Court ball of fifty years before.

'You haven't told me your name,' he said, accepting the wine.

'Purity. I'm your Aunt Purity,' she said at once. 'My father was a great Puritan, you know. Hard and cool and unforgiving! No cakes and ale for us, I can tell you.'

'And your mother?'

'Your grandmother,' she reminded him. 'Oh, she died when I was born, but I'm told she was gentle and comely. She was part Romany and my father despised her for that. The marriage wasn't a happy one.'

'But there were children.'

'Begotten in an unloving bed, and there are worse fates,' she said wryly. 'Five of us were born and all gone now except me.'

'Have I any cousins?'

She shook her white head.

'There were, I thought, none left except me,' she said. 'It seems odd that Luther should have wed. He was the wildest of us all, forever looking towards the horizon.'

'He married late in life,' Petroc told her.

'My mother was a Cornishwoman, a Penhallow. She's dead now too.'

'And you've come up into Yorkshire,

to see your old auntie.'

'To see the house where my father was born,' he said.

'We were all born here,' she said. 'And soon I'll die here. The winters tell me it won't be long, but the summer comes and bids me wait awhile. I'll never leave this house again. Oh, when I was a young woman, I visited London and saw King Charles. Tall and black, bowing to the people who watched him eating his dinner in Westminster Hall. That was a long time past and the love of living was strong in me. You'll stay here for a while, won't you, to bear an old woman company?'

'If I'll be no trouble.'

'Lord forbid that the day should ever dawn when a man is a trouble to me!' she exclaimed in a sprightly fashion. 'Let me show you over the house. It's in good order, though I've let the garden go to seed.'

'Has it always been in the Makin family?' he asked, rising.

'No, my father bought the place

when he married my mother. It had stood empty for years. My aunt told me once there were rumours that a witch had lived here. Some folk say the same of me these days, so I beg leave to doubt if t'other was a witch either! Come with me.'

She was bustling out of the parlour into a second, larger hall out of which stairs led to a wide landing and then divided into twin staircases at left and right.

'There's another parlour here,' she said, opening a door at the other side of the hall. 'It was built on after the original house. A fine big room for entertaining, but nobody comes here now.'

'It's a lovely room,' he said, and had a fleeting moment of anger.

Goda would have lifted her voice in song to have been blessed with such a room, but she had lived all her days in tiny, smoky apartments. All this was wasted on one old woman. The whole house cried out for tripping footsteps and laughing voices.

'The master bedroom is up here,' she informed him, turning left on the landing. 'My father used it, but it's been kept empty since.'

It was a large, low ceilinged room hung with faded tapestry. Bolted to the floor against one wall was an iron-bound chest. Aunt Purity, catching his glance, said sharply.

'Don't be imagining there's a fortune there! I sold off the sheep years since, but the profit was small. Enough to see me comfortably into the next world and leave Emma something for her dowry.'

But the house was solid, many of its furnishings old and valuable, and the garden fairly extensive.

'I have three thousand pounds of my own,' he said, 'so I'm not craving your savings, aunt.'

'Three thousand! Have you been robbing rich widows?' she demanded.

'I've spent fifteen years voyaging and spent little,' he said.

The money could be used to buy

sheep, employ more servants to clean the house and replant the garden.

'The two rooms up there,' she said, 'were used by Aunt Hepzibah. She was father's sister and died a spinster. These two are mine. I sleep in one and wait in the other.'

'Wait?'

'For James Rodale — or death, or whatever comes knocking in the middle of the night. I'll tell you about him one day.'

The stairs twisted up to another corridor. She waved her skinny hand towards them.

'There are two guest rooms up there, but we never have guests.'

'I'm here,' he reminded her.

'But not as a guest. I've a notion you'll stay. If you like you can use the master bedroom.'

'It's haunted, I suppose?'

She gave a shrill cackle of amusement.

'The only ghost around this place is me! Oh, there is something though

111

— not a ghost but a priest hole, from the bad old days when Catholics were regarded as traitors.'

'They still are, in some quarters.'

'Ah, well, I've no interest in politics and less in religion!' Aunt Purity said. 'You'll be interested in this though.'

She returned to the master bedroom and, opening a door, disclosed a steep, narrow staircase.

'Built into the wall,' she told him, 'behind the chimney in the small parlour. The panel next to the front door slides back. But the priest hole proper is under the top stair. You can stand a man down there — not for very long else he'd suffocate, but for long enough to fool a searcher. I've often wondered if anyone ever hid there.'

The room had grown cooler, the sunlight retreating, Petroc shivered.

'I left my horse down by the river,' he said. 'I'll put her in the stables. You do have stables?'

'And a barn,' she nodded, 'beyond the orchard. There are no horses there

112

now, though there is a small carriage. Out-of-date like everything else. I'll get supper while you're gone.'

'I'm hungry.' He glanced at the concealed stairs and decided to use the main one.

At the kitchen door she laid her hand on his arm and looked up at him.

'You will come back, won't you?' she asked. 'When folks leave, one can never be sure. I'm so weary of waiting.'

'Ten minutes,' he promised, and swung away into the tall grass.

It was a relief to be out in the air again. He drew in a deep breath of fragrance and hastened his steps. The horse stood patiently, its head drooping a little. He unleashed it and led it back up the slope into the garden again. Even in such a short time the house had assumed an aspect of familiarity. He stared at it for a few moments, trying to imagine how his father must have felt as he left for the last time, riding away from the Puritan father, turning his back on the prosperity of the only life he had ever known. And in the end the sea had taken him.

The stables were not in good repair, but there was hay there, and he drew a pail of water from the well outside for the animal to drink.

Coming back into the house he found his aunt bustling about in the kitchen. Old as she was she was still spry, or perhaps his arrival had given her energy.

'Supper will be ready soon,' she said cheerfully over her shoulder. 'I make certain I eat one good meal a day. Emma brings what I need from market.

'Do we eat here?' He glanced at the dais on which a table and chairs were placed.

'In the parlour. It's more friendly there,' she returned, 'and while we eat you can tell me all about yourself. I want to know how my brother fared, how he lived and died.'

'You ask for half a century in an hour,' he said, taking the heavy tray from her and going into the parlour.

'I shall make you spin out the tale night after night,' she said following him, with wine jug and goblets.

'There's little enough to tell,' Petroc said. 'My father spoke very little of his early life. I think he'd had it in mind to travel, but the farm was a challenge, and he wrestled with it all his life.'

'And your mother? What was she like? Beautiful?'

'She was lame,' he said, briefly because the memory gave him pain. 'She was pisky touched as they say in Cornwall, and so didn't go among folk very often. But she was beautiful for all that, and sang like a bird.'

'And died you say?'

'While I was away at sea.' He had no wish to reopen a too recent wound.

'And Luther was drowned? How does a farmer come to be drowned?'

'The profits from the farm were low,' he explained. 'He had a boat and fished from him, and we used to set lobster traps. He went out before a storm one afternoon and never came back. Only

115

the wreckage of his boat was washed ashore.'

'And yet you went to sea yourself?' She bit into a piece of pie and fixed bright eyes upon him.

'I craved adventure,' he said.

'And your Cornish farm?'

'I've nothing to hold me in Cornwall. I travelled north to see if any of the Makins were still alive, to look at the place where my father was born.'

'And you will stay awhile?'

He nodded at the saddle bags he had dropped in the corner.

'My profits are there. I've a mind to employ them to good purpose, buy a flock of sheep, settle into wedlock.'

'At Ladymoon Manor?'

'If there's a future for me here?' He raised his brow questioningly.

'I've no family left except you,' she said promptly. 'I didn't even know that you existed until a little time ago.'

'You will need proof of identity,' he said. 'My mother's relatives were never close to us but they'd vouch for me. I have certificates of my marine status too.'

'You look like Luther,' she said simply. 'Bigger than he used to be, but with the same eyes and hair. I've no need of further proof.'

'Yet you thought I was someone else when you saw me in the garden.'

Colour ran up beneath her faded skin and her mouth trembled.

'You thought I was James Rodale,' he persisted.

'It was foolish,' she said in a low voice. 'James is certainly dead by now, for he was almost thirty years older than I am. But years are such silly things, some fast, some slow, and how can we hope to measure time.'

'Was he your lover? Tell me about him,' he urged.

'He was the only man I ever loved,' she said.

'And?'

'And there's nothing more to tell, save that he left me. Nearly fifty years I've waited, at first in the hope he

117

would return, later on because there was nothing else to do. Family dead, house empty, myself growing older.'

'A lonely life,' he said, touched again by pity.

'I had the house.' she told him, 'and the moon rising over the river. The house is built upon the foundations of a Roman dwelling house, did you know? The little room at the back of the hall has an original mosaic floor, we used to have family prayers in that room, and once when I was a girl — I cannot recall exactly what occurred, save that I seemed to be in a temple and a man was attacking it. It's possible the event really happened, for barbarians certainly invaded these parts and drove the Roman settlers away.'

'There are always barbarians,' Petroc said.

'And the house quiet and still,' she mused. 'Waiting, as I wait, and nobody coming. Year after year, summer after winter, spring and autumn shading the seasons of birth and decay.'

She was, he thought uneasily, more than a little crazy. Or perhaps she was merely old and had been too much alone, for an instant later she put aside her plate and rose, saying briskly, 'I'll need to put clean linen in the master bedroom. Mind, I've kept it aired and sweetened, so you'll sleep well. No, stay and finish your meal. I like to see a man with a hearty appetite!'

He leaned back, swallowing the last of the pie, washing it down with a draught of the wine.

His grandfather, Puritan though he might have been, had certainly laid down an excellent cellar, and the meal, though warmed over, had been tasty. He wondered if Emma Rowe did the cooking as well as the shopping.

The sun was sinking lower, the rooms cooling, faint shadows gathering in the corners. He put down his glass and went out into the hall again. He'd bed down the horse for the night, and the next morning he'd ride to York and establish his credit there. He'd also to see to it that Aunt Purity made a will. If he used his money in order to make Ladymoon Manor more prosperous then it was only wise to ensure that the house would eventually come to him.

A girl was hurrying through the orchard. He had a glimpse of her between the creeper hung trunks of the laden fruit trees, and a few moments later she came into full view, her flowered skirts held clear of the brambles, a straw bonnet on her fair head.

She hesitated for a moment and then came towards him, a smile hovering about her lips.

'Sir, is Mistress Makin sick? I was afeared when I saw a stranger that she'd been taken bad!'

'She's perfectly well. You must be — ' He frowned slightly as he eyed her, for though she was small she was plump and her dress revealed mature contours.

'Emma Rowe, sir. I come over most days to work at the house.'

'*Little* Emma! I fancied from the way

my aunt spoke of you, that you were no more than a child!' he exclaimed.

'I'm past twenty,' she began, and interrupted herself with, 'You said 'aunt', sir. Is Mistress Makin your aunt?'

'I am Petroc Makin, her brother's son.'

'Would that be her brother, Luther?' she enquired. 'The one who quarrelled with the family long ago?'

'He was my father,' he nodded.

'And now you've come back for a visit?'

'I hope to settle here,' he told her.

'At Ladymoon?' Her face lit into a smile that transformed her features into beauty. 'Oh, sir, that's the best news I've heard in a twelvemonth! I get right fretted about Mistress Makin sometimes, all alone in that great house! I've offered to sleep in but she'll not hear of it.'

'Do you come over every evening?' he enquired.

'Why, it's only a step of a mile or

121

two,' she assured him cheerfully. 'Nothing at all to speak about.'

'You live at home then?'

'With my parents and my two brothers, sir. Mistress Makin had the house built for my grandparents, you know. She was always good to our family.'

'It's a pity that it was not better appreciated then,' he said, looking at the unweeded garden.

'My brothers are lazy,' she said, flushing, 'and since the flocks were sold off, my father's been his own man. He does try to help, sir, but Mistress Makin is old and she can be difficult sometimes.'

'Yet you come every day.'

'We'll all be old one day,' she said placidly. 'It will be a hard world when nobody wants us. Have you had anything to eat yet, sir? I cook for two or three days at once but she sometimes forgets to eat.'

'We both ate well tonight,' he assured her. 'My compliments to the cook also.'

'I like to cook and keep house,' she said, blushing again.

Her face was extraordinarily mobile, expressions flitting across it as swiftly as sunshine following shower. Her skin was exquisite too, clear and unmarked by pox, and her eyes were of so clear a blue that the whites seemed tinged with it.

'Was there anything more you wanted, sir?' she asked.

He became aware that he was staring at her.

'Nothing.' He bowed slightly as if she were not a servant.

'Mistress Makin will probably be glad of your help though. She's getting my room ready.'

'All by herself!' Emma gave him a reproachful look. 'She'll do herself an injury like as not, trying to turn the mattress! Excuse me, sir.'

She darted past him into the house and when she had gone the garden seemed more lonely than it had been before.

6

Petroc stepped out into the garden and drew several deep breaths of contentment. It was, he considered, good to be alive on such a day. All around him the gardens flaunted the orderly beauty of trim lawns, clipped hedges, herb bordered paths and fragrant rose beds.

On the other side of the hedge the trees raised green decked heads up into the blue sky. There had been an excellent yield of apples and pears the previous autumn and this season promised to be even better. At the other side row after row of vegetables marched along carefully weeded furrows of rich brown earth, sheltered from the moorland wind by thick bushes of currant and gooseberry and bramble.

Behind the house were the newly repaired stables where his two hunters and three mares were lodged, and next to the new threshing barn was the shed where six milking cows had wintered. Further afield, grazing on the common land, sheep bore the half-moon brand above the letter M. The profits from the sale of the spring fleeces had provided a new well, bored down near the kitchen door and making the work of the household much less onerous.

The house itself gleamed, the panelled walls rubbed with beeswax, new Indian rugs covering the floors, copper glowing against the white-washed walls of kitchen and scullery and stillroom.

Flowers were arranged in parlour and drawing room, and a handsome consignment of leather-bound books had recently been arranged in newly acquired bookcases. Ladymoon Manor was the house of a cultured and respected gentleman. A house, but not quite a home. Only Aunt Purity sat sewing by the parlour fire or fingered the beribboned lute in the drawing room, and at night he slept alone in the velvet curtained bed of the master bedroom.

It was time for him to wed. For five years he had worked to establish himself as a responsible citizen. He had bought his livestock with care, beating down the prices to a figure that would enhance his reputation as a shrewd businessman. For the same reason he had employed local labour for the rebuilding and repairs to the property; he had hired servants from York, paying them fair wages and putting Emma Rowe in charge as housekeeper.

In recognition of her status she now had the use of the two small rooms where old Hepzibah Makin had once lived out her spinster existence.

Emma was coming towards him across the garden, a basket on her arm. It occurred to him that he never saw her without some burden in her hand. The basket contained blackberries today and there were juice stains about her mouth.

'We ought to make you whistle while

you're gathering the fruit. Emma,' he smiled, 'or the entire crop will be gone before one pie is made.'

'There are more than the whole world could eat,' she said placidly. 'I'm hoping to fill the stock cupboards with jelly and preserves, and Cook has a famous recipe for bramble butter she wants to try. Will you have some pie this evening, Master Petroc?'

'I'll not be in for supper,' he said briefly. 'I'm riding to York.'

'Oh!' A faint shadow crossed her face and was gone at once as she smiled brightly. 'Will you be home tomorrow or do you stay longer?'

'Tomorrow, if my business is concluded in time.'

'I'll make pie for tomorrow,' Emma promised. 'Ride safely, sir.'

He turned to watch her as she went indoors. She was a comely young woman, too plump for her height but with that exquisite skin and those brilliant blue eyes a female worth watching. He had been tempted in her direction several times over the years, but he had been careful to refrain from treating her with anything warmer than a cool friendliness. Emma was a virtuous woman and would expect marriage to follow seduction, and he had never lost sight of his own ambition. The woman who would bear his children must be a lady of quality with a handsome dowry. But Emma was a comely woman for all that.

He sighed briefly, his contentment unsettled. It was certainly high time for him to make an offer for Dorothy Allston. He had been visiting her for over a year and believed she regarded him with favour. Certainly it would be convenient to have a woman in his bed whenever he desired one rather than having to ride over to one of the discreet York establishments where single gentlemen were accommodated. And Dorothy was comely too, her brown hair fluffed up into a chignon, her voice languid with little trace of a Yorkshire accent.

Her father, Sir John, was a distant kinsman of the Earl of Derwentwater, and his only daughter had been very gently reared, with a French governess and an Italian drawing-master.

Thinking of Dorothy had roused his energy. He took another satisfied look about the luxuriant garden, and went briskly up the path. He would ride alone, as he usually did, relying on sword and a brace of pistols to discourage footpads.

The ride was, as he had expected, uneventful. As he entered the narrow cobbled streets of the city several people recognised him and doffed their hats, or bowed as they stood aside to allow him passage. He bowed back courteously, his greetings polite but brief. He was aware of the things that were said about him.

'A Cornishman from nowhere, but a nephew to old Mistress Makin for all that, and Yorkshire in his dealings.'

Having stabled his mount he walked the remaining fifty yards to the house he had acquired at low cost a couple of years before. The building was a narrow, two storey one squeezed between two larger ones like a thin girl between two buxom matrons.

In this house he could conduct the business that gave him not only added income but the pleasure of knowing that, behind the scenes, he wielded a certain power. As he kept no servant here there were none to gossip about the hours he kept, or to speculate the identities of the men who sometimes visited him under cover of darkness.

He let himself in and went up the narrow stairs into the bedroom. It was sparsely furnished but he seldom used the bed for more than a few hours. He kept a change of clothing here and on this evening dressed with particular care for his supper engagement with the Allstons. His coat of pinkish buff fitted closely over the brown waistcoat and flared over matching breeches. Ruffles of cream lawn edged his shirt and his low-heeled shoes were buckled in silver.

He wore his own plentiful hair tied back loosely with a brown ribbon, and his low crowned tricorn was edged with silver braid. Glancing at himself in the mirror he decided, without passion, that he looked very different from the gangling lad who had struck a bargain with Sir Taverne Bostock.

His toilet complete he left the house and strolled through the city at a leisurely pace. The Allstons had a comfortable house near the Minster, a building he supposed was modest by London standards, but which displayed a luxury that even Ladymoon Manor could not match.

He was admitted at once into the long narrow drawing room that over-looked the river. The fierce afternoon heat had cooled into an airy sunset and patterns of lacy gold marked the shadowed floor. Dorothy's green skirt was splashed with the gold, and the trinkets on her fingers winked and gleamed as she extended a languid hand.

131

'Master Makin, we feared you had forgotten the invitation,' she reproached. 'No word for nigh on three weeks! I began to think I had offended you.'

'Only by being too beautiful,' he responded, kissing her hand and accepting a chair near the sofa on which she reclined.

'Offend you by being too beautiful!' she echoed, raising plucked brows. 'Pray, sir, how could I possibly do that?'

'By driving all thoughts out of my head, so that my business takes twice as long to perform, and I am forced to delay my visit.'

'La, sir! what fustian you talk! You run on so fast my poor head is quite bewildered,' Dorothy said.

'As you bewilder my senses,' he said gallantly. The girl was an empty-headed fool, of course, for all her fine education, but she was beautiful and healthy despite her fad for lying about on sofas.

'Tell me what you've been doing with

yourself these past few weeks,' he invited.

'Sulking,' she said promptly.

'Sulking, and you a woman grown!' he exclaimed. 'That's hard to credit.'

'At least you recognise that I'm a woman grown,' she pouted. 'My father treats me as if I were a child — or a prisoner, for he keeps me close penned in this dull place and will not let me go to Court.'

'To be leered at by German George? No, my girl, I will not! Master Makin, your servant, sir.'

Sir John Allston had entered and brought with him a welcome feeling of the outdoors. Unlike his daughter he was a stocky individual with a handsome, high coloured face. His coat of dull red clashed with the delicate colours of the furnishings, but he seemed blissfully unaware of the fact as he shook hands briskly.

'You'll stay over in York for a few days, I hope,' he said cordially. 'We see very little of you these days, I regret to say. However, as I tell my discontented Dorothy, we cannot all be dancing attendance upon the ladies all the time! How is your aunt?'

'More frail than she used to be,' he said regretfully. 'She seems to live more in the past these days, and constantly muddles me up with my father. But Emma takes many of the burdens of the household on her own shoulders.'

'The inestimable Emma,' Sir John smiled. 'If you're not careful someone will whisk her up the aisle and you'll have to find another housekeeper.'

'Rather than that I'd marry her myself,' Petroc said, laughing to show he didn't mean it.

'You might do worse, lad,' Sir John said heartily. 'Didn't you tell me once that your father wed a poor fisher girl? And from what you've said she proved a good wife and mother.'

Petroc nodded briefly, not wishing to talk about it. Though he was not ashamed of his origins he felt strongly that the man he had become had little in common with the lad who had listened to Goda sing down the moon.

'I shall never be a wife or a mother,' Dorothy said plaintively, 'for I shall die of boredom before the opportunity to wed arises!'

'If you ever choose to visit Ladymoon Manor,' Petroc said, 'we'd try to entertain you, though it might not vie with the excitements of Court.'

'There is precious little excitement at the Court these days,' said Sir John. 'All is heaviness, and coarse lewdness is mistaken there for wit. There is not even overmuch cleanliness among the German sycophants who prowl about the throne.'

'The king does not, I understand, speak much English?'

'Not a word, not a single word,' Sir John said. 'One might have thought that he would have had the grace to learn the language of the country he has been invited to rule over.'

'You drink to the king over the water then?' Petroc enquired.

'To His Majesty King James the Third of the House of Stuart,' Sir John said.

'Isn't it possible that the child born to Mary of Modena did not survive and was substituted by another?' Petroc asked.

'Political bitchery, stirred up by those who hated the Stuarts and wished to put an end to the hopes of a peaceful succession,' Sir John snapped.

'Are we going to discuss monstrous dull subjects all evening or are we going to talk about more interesting things?' Dorothy said.

'Forgive me, Mistress Allston, I fear that when politics come in at the window gaiety flies out of the door,' Petroc said. 'Tell me if you have learned any new pieces. If you have I shall take it as a great favour if you consent to entertain us later.'

Mollified, Dorothy gave him one of her sweetest smiles, her eyes crinkling attractively at the corners. Petroc, rising and leaning to help her to her feet,

136

smelled the perfume she wore and was conscious again of his senses quickening. She was a comely woman, he decided again, and he would be a fool to delay any longer.

Supper passed amiably. The food was well cooked and subtly spiced, the wine chilled, the fruit prettily sugared and garnished with clotted cream. Under its influence Dorothy blossomed, her smile sparkling, her narrow face flushed and lively in the light of the candles that glowed in the silver candelabra on the white clothed table.

After supper Dorothy excused herself and drifted into the parlour that led out of the dining room. From time to time the notes of a spinet tinkled to them as they sat over their tankards of port.

'Mistress Dorothy is a charming young lady,' Petroc said, raising his tankard towards the door.

'But the music distracts from serious conversation,' Sir John said. 'Close the door quietly so that the dear girl is not offended, and come and sit down again then. There is something to discuss.'

He did as he was bade and resumed his place at the table. The dishes had been cleared and the servants dismissed, the windows shuttered against the chill of the evening and the fire banked up with fresh-sawn apple logs. For some reason their scent reminded him of Emma.

'You wished to discuss something with me, and I with you,' he said, banishing Emma from his mind. 'I hope our aims will meet and match, sir.'

'No reason why you should have any fear about that,' Sir John said, moving his chair slightly and stretching his legs to the blaze. 'You and I see eye to eye in most things. I've always admired effort and industry, and I like a self-made man, as well as any.'

'I hope I've made some progress in establishing myself,' Petroc said formally.

'You've established a reputation for fair dealing; that's certain,' Sir John said. 'Ladymoon Manor is a handsome house, they tell me. You may take credit for that, sir. In fact I've had it in mind to ride over for some time and visit you.'

'And neither you nor Mistress Dorothy need to wait for an invitation,' Petroc said.

'Very civil of you, my dear sir.' Sir John raised his own tankard and inclined his head.

'It is of Mistress Dorothy I wish to talk,' Petroc said.

'Of my girl? What of her?'

'She is a very lovely young woman,' Petroc said, 'and of age.'

'She came of age in May,' her father said. 'Not that I consider the number of years a female has lived to be any indication of her good sense! My wife was a very fetching baggage, pretty as a rose, with less intelligence than my horse! But Dorothy is not, I flatter myself, completely empty-headed. She has elegance and style, and might be guided into commonsense.'

'Unless she goes to Court,' Petroc ventured.

'I've no intention of allowing her to travel south,' Sir John said.

'It would be better if you were to allow her to wed,' Petroc said. 'A female is all the better for a husband, they say.'

'And say truly, sir! My girl will make an admirable wife if the right husband may be selected,' Sir John said.

'Sir, that is the reason for my wishing to speak to you,' Petroc said swiftly. 'It has been in my mind to wed these past months, and my choice has fallen upon your lovely daughter, Sir John. She does not regard me with disfavour, and I — I have a very deep affection for her.'

'You and my daughter.' Sir John set down his tankard and stared at his younger companion.

'I desire to make an offer for her hand,' Petroc said.

'Do you indeed? And what is your precise offer?' Sir John enquired.

'Ladymoon Manor is a handsome house, as you said yourself. Mistress

Dorothy would have a very comfortable home, within riding distance of yourself in York. There would be no danger of her rushing to London.'

'There is no danger of that anyway,' Sir John said sharply. 'Dorothy is an obedient daughter and strives to please me.'

'Of course, sir, but you have said she will be happy when she is a wife and mother.'

'Indeed I did, but you cannot imagine that I was thinking of you as her prospective bridegroom!' Sir John exclaimed.

'I am of good family,' Petroc began.

'On your father's side. Your mother was a Cornish peasant.'

'I've never hidden the fact,' Petroc said quietly.

Inside him a cold, sick feeling was rising up. Sir John looked nothing like Sir Taverne but both had the same easy arrogance of manner that comes after centuries of breeding.

'I give you every credit for your

honesty,' he said now. 'Indeed it has pleased me to admit you to friendship, to watch your progress in society. But that is a very different thing from greeting you as a prospective son-in-law.'

'I have a deep affection for Mistress Dorothy,' Petroc repeated.

'Almost as great as the affection you have for her dowry?' Sir John asked dryly and held up his hand to check any intended protest. 'I don't blame you, sir. A man who loves a penniless woman is a fool. Oh, I'm aware your father did just that and I've no doubt that your mother was an admirable woman, but in worldly terms he did himself no good by wedding her. You are very wise to seek a bride with property.'

'I am not penniless myself.' He spoke stiffly, holding down his anger.

'And will doubtless grow richer,' Sir John said. 'You may count upon me to further your business interests in any way open to me. But, my dear fellow, weddings are not simply a question of affection or of dowry. It is a matter of breeding, and the Allstons have been connected with the Lords of Northumberland for centuries. One of my ancestors fell at Agincourt, sir. Another was one of the first Merchant Adventurers. The Makins cannot match that, I fear.'

'I fear they can't,' Petroc said.

'Then we'll talk no more of the matter,' Sir John said, 'I am flattered by the interest you show in my girl, sir, and I admire your good sense in talking to me first. That shows a gentlemanly spirit, sir.'

'I thank you.' Petroc drank, the port stinging his throat.

'What I did wish to talk to you about,' Sir John said, 'was the possibility of our coming to an arrangement of a different nature. You are aware that King James plans to regain his father's throne?'

'I've heard rumours,' Petroc said cautiously.

143

'More than rumours,' said the other. 'Scotland is loyal to the Stuarts, and more men than you could count will not rest until that prince of Hanover is thrust back to his German Duchy.'

'You spoke of an arrangement,' Petroc said.

'So I did. You breed sheep, Master Makin.'

'I have a flock.'

'And you take an interest in the rearing of them. You ride out often over the moors.'

'That's true, but I don't see — '

'You know the ways across the moor, the hidden paths that avoid the main towns.'

'I've made myself familiar with the land.'

'And having been at sea can draw up maps and plot weather charts I've no doubt?'

'I have done work of that nature,' Petroc said.

'Those who come over the borders

will march south-west through Liverpool, gaining support as they come,' Sir John said. 'Eventually the loyalists will swing south-east and clear the road to London. There will be others already there to close the Stuart pincers and grip German George by his fat neck.'

'And those others?'

'Will travel along unfrequented paths. They will pass unobserved.'

'Provided with reliable maps, I suppose.'

'For which you would be handsomely paid, at very little risk.'

'It's a tempting offer,' Petroc said slowly.

'You'll agree to it?'

'I'll consider it most carefully,' Petroc said. 'I am grateful for the trust you place in me.'

'I know men and am seldom wrong in my estimation of character.' Sir John said. 'You'll take another drink before we join Mistress Dorothy?'

His voice was friendly, but he had used his daughter's formal title,

145

reminding the other of the social barrier between them. So far, but no further, Petroc thought with bitterness, just as it had been long ago in Cornwall when he was a boy and had loved Catriona Bostock.

'You'll excuse me if I take my leave now,' he said aloud. 'I have much to think about. Will you make my apologies to Mistress Dorothy? I'll leave by the side door.'

'You are a trifle downcast by my earlier refusal. That's to be expected,' Sir John said. 'I hope it will not alter the friendship that exists between us?'

'Naturally not, but I am, as you say, downcast by your refusal.'

'Tush! You're no green lad to sigh over a lost love!' Sir John exclaimed, clapping him on the shoulder. 'And you're shrewd enough not to turn your back on a possible source of income. And we none of us owe any loyalty to German George.'

'True, my dear sir.' He bowed and smiled, his face expressing just the right

146

proportions of regret and cupidity.

In the side passage he took his hat and gloves from the servant and stood, outwardly patient, while his dress sword was buckled on. Through an unshuttered window he could still hear the notes of the spinet. Empty, tinkling notes which said nothing to his heart.

He smiled briefly, holding himself a little more erect than usual as the garden door was opened for him. The garden ran down to the river under a moonlit sky, but he turned briskly from contemplation of its beauty.

He would have to hurry back if his report were to be ready for the agent whom he expected at midnight. The government would be most interested in the full extent of Jacobite involvement in Yorkshire.

7

'So that is the end of my part in the affair!'

Petroc spoke aloud, rubbing his hands together. Everything in his opinion had turned out splendidly. James Stuart had gone back to the Continent with his tail between his legs and the crown of England further from his grasp than ever. The rebels were scattered without having ventured further south than Preston, and for the time being, German George could sit comfortably upon the throne.

'Such a terrible thing,' Emma said in distress. 'It's all over the neighbourhood that Sir John Allston is taken for treason. One would never have imagined such a state of affairs.'

'Men are not always what they seem,' Petroc said.

'But you will do what you can?' she

asked trustingly. 'They say that Mistress Dorothy is heartbroken and quite alone. There is even talk of her being arrested too for complicity in her father's plots!'

'Mere gossip!' Petroc had mocked, and she had not pursued the subject.

But he had ridden to York as soon as he possibly could, and now sat in the upper room of his tiny house, gazing at the ledgers before him. Here, in neatly inked figures, were the records of his financial transactions over the past five years. There were the details of flocks bought and wool sold, of repairs to the property, of crops sown, of horses acquired. And in the small ledger were the initialled entries of money received for services rendered to the new monarchy. Those proceeds had been paid in gold, together with the money he had received from the sale of his York house, now rested in his bank where the ledgers would also be kept. He was, he decided, as he gathered his books together, right to be pleased by his success. Not many men had come so far so fast, and his most recent service might, he had been assured, lead to his being appointed a Justice of the Peace.

He smiled, thoughtfully smoothing the panels of his flared brown coat. His reflection in the glass was that of a handsome man of mature years and intelligent aspect. Too intelligent to be content with the life of a farming squire for ever! He would, as soon as he was safely wed, begin the study of law. It would mean many years of hard work and study, but he believed himself to be equal to the task, and the ambition to be greater than the woman who had rejected him was stronger than ever.

A little later, having deposited the ledgers in the bank vaults, he walked slowly to the Allston house. As he had anticipated the windows were shuttered and two guards on duty at the door demanded his business.

'For with Sir John bound for trial in London and the place still under search we have to know who comes in and out, sir,' one of the men said.

'You have your duty to do,' Petroc approved, handing them the written authority from the Sheriff with which he had furnished himself.

'Yes, sir, but it's a hard one,' the man said. 'Sir John was well respected in the city and his daughter near prostrate with grief.'

'Treason is a terrible thing,' Petroc agreed. 'You'll have the carriage brought round in a few minutes.'

'And provided with a few comforts for her journey,' the man nodded. 'She'll be best out of it, poor lady.'

'Indeed she will.' Petroc moved on into the house. Dorothy lay on her usual sofa but no volume of poetry or illustrated song sheet dangled from her slim fingers, and her hair was pulled to the top of her head and pinned there in an unfashionable coil. As Petroc came in she turned eyes swollen with weeping towards him.

'Master Petroc — may I call you

that? So kind of you to come!'

'Why, mistress, I thought you would have been surrounded by friends!' he exclaimed.

'Friends indeed!' Dorothy cried, her voice thinning into petulance. 'Fair weather friends! Nobody has been near since my father was taken.'

'They don't wish to be seen to be associated with a — suspected rebel,' Petroc said.

'I cannot believe it,' Dorothy said. 'I know my father had no love for the new monarch, but that he should be involved in treasonable practice is — I cannot believe it.'

'It seems there is little doubt since he is committed for trial in London,' Petroc said.

'They questioned me,' she said tearfully. 'Over and over they asked questions about my father's affairs but I know nothing of business. They searched the house too and took away papers and letters. And most of the servants have given notice.'

'The fire needs mending,' he frowned, 'and your gown is too thin for the season, though it becomes you vastly.'

'This old thing?' She glanced down at her low-necked dress of lilac and purple, the ghost of a smile touching her mouth. 'I put on the first thing to hand, and this is three years old. It was always a particular favourite of my father.'

'You must try not to dwell upon his present trouble,' Petroc advised. 'You have not seen him?'

'I was confined to the house by order of the Sheriff,' she said. 'I have seen nothing of him since his arrest. Now they tell me he is to stand trial in London. They will find him guilty and cut off his head and then what will become of me?'

'That is the whole purpose of my errand,' he said. 'I came to offer you the protection of my home, my dear.'

'Protection? I don't understand,' she said helplessly.

'It's very simple.' He looked round and, seeing a cloak draped over a chair, brought it to her and wrapped her about.

'Protection?' she said again. 'Do they mean to arrest me too? I know nothing of such matters as rebellion or treason.'

'Of course you don't,' he soothed, 'but you may not be believed for all that. Why, even your name will be against you, for Allston will be connected by implication if nothing else, with the rebel cause!'

'But I cannot help my name,' she said in terror, 'and I cannot tell them what I don't know, or confess to what I've never done.'

'I am offering you the protection of my home and of my name,' Petroc said. 'It has long been in my mind to offer for your hand, but I held off, knowing my own humble beginnings. Now I feel there may be a chance for me to help you and obtain my desire.'

'To wed me? But will it not be unwise for you to seek a connection with me at this moment?' she asked in surprise.

'My own loyalty is not in question,' he said, 'and my marriage to you would raise you beyond suspicion.'

'I cannot think clearly.' Huddled in the cloak she stared up at him, tears beading her lashes. 'I would have to see my father and ask his permission, beg his advice.'

'You would not be allowed to visit him, I fear,' he said sorrowfully.

'Then what am I to do?' she pleaded.

'I cannot speak through the mouth of another man,' he said carefully, 'but I have known your father for sufficient time to be able to say that he loves you most dearly, and that your present situation can only add to his worries.'

'I cannot tell, I cannot tell,' she repeated.

'Dorothy — may I call you so? — you do not dislike me, do you?' he asked.

'No, indeed!' she said swiftly. 'I have always considered you as a friend, as more than a friend.'

155

'Marriage is but a short step from that,' he said.

'And a necessary one? You do consider it necessary?'

'If your father were here I believe that he would consider it imperative,' he assured her.

'Then we will have to be married.' She drew the cloak higher and said in a small voice, 'I'm sure I'm very grateful to you, Master Petroc.'

'You will like Ladymoon Manor,' he reassured her. 'It is not so fine as this house, but it's a lovely place for all that, and the air on the moors is bracing. Aunt Purity will certainly welcome you, for she would have loved a daughter of her own.'

'I am confined here,' she reminded him. 'How could such a marriage be contrived with guards on the door?'

'I took the liberty of obtaining a safe conduct for you from the Sheriff,' he revealed. 'You are free to leave, provided you are with me, under my protection.'

156

'Then we could marry?'

'At Otley, in the church there. The minister is a sound man and a friend of mine. Tomorrow morning might suit very well. You will have had a good night's sleep by then and Emma can attend to your toilet.'

'Your housekeeper?'

'A good faithful soul,' Petroc said. 'She will be of very great help to you.'

'I would need to pack,' Dorothy said, running a distracted hand through her hair. Limp curls fell in disarray over her temples.

'Bring your jewel case under your cloak,' he said. 'Your other dresses can be sent on when the guards on the house are removed.'

'I cannot ride so far,' she said pitifully. 'I've not eaten all day and my hair is a mess.'

'Go and tidy it,' he said patiently, drawing her to her feet. 'Bring your jewels down. We'd not want them to fall into the wrong hands, would we? I'll

157

have your father's carriage brought round.'

'You're very masterful,' she said, leaning against him for an instant. 'I begin to feel more secure.'

'Hurry then and we'll be on our way,' he said.

There was nothing of Catriona's proud dignity in Dorothy Allston, he thought gloomily as she hurried out of the room, but she had breeding and her father had placed her out of his reach. That last consideration weighed most heavily with him.

'Master Makin, there's a gentleman here to see Mistress Allston.'

One of the guards was at the door beckoning forward an elderly gentleman whose bag-wig and high stock betokened a member of the legal profession.

'Master Gibson, good-day to you,' Petroc bowed cordially. 'This is a terrible affair.'

'Terrible indeed, and I fear the outcome for my client,' the lawyer said.

'He is to be taken to London early tomorrow and will stand trial there.'

'So I heard. The king may be merciful.'

'One hopes so.' Master Gibson's face expressed a complete absence of hope. 'Sir John wishes to see his daughter. I am here to escort her to the prison.'

'My dear sir, Mistress Dorothy is still prostrate with shock,' Petroc reproached. 'I am taking her back to Ladymoon Manor with me at once to see if fresh air and quiet will restore her nerves.'

'She is going with you?'

'We are to be wed. It has been understood between us for some time, but I feel further delay might be unwise.'

'But Mistress Dorothy is not in danger of arrest, my dear sir,' the lawyer said. 'It is clear she's a mere child, knowing nothing of business.'

'And is a loving child to be taken into a prison to see a parent on his way to trial for treason?' Petroc reproached.

'The experience would be devastating.'

'Her father will be deeply disappointed,' Master Gibson said.

'And as a compassionate man, as well as an attorney, you have no wish to deliver such a message. I can understand that.'

'I am not even permitted to travel down to London and represent him in the Court there,' the lawyer said. 'I cannot blame him, for I was unable to stop the preliminary hearing from going further. I hoped — '

'As Mistress Dorothy's betrothed I could never allow her to be subjected to such a meeting,' Petroc said. 'I will send a message to Sir John if you wish, to save your having to return to the prison yourself.'

'That would be most civil of you, sir.' The man's face had brightened. 'It was not an errand I'd care to make. Sir John can be most forceful. He even declared that if he is finally condemned he will take others with him.'

'I'll write at once and send it by one

160

of the guards,' Petroc said. 'You'll excuse my not offering you refreshment, but under the circumstances — '

'I quite understand. You will give my regards to Mistress Dorothy, my good wishes for her recovery? She is fortunate that you are here.'

He bowed and went into the hall again, his head bent as if sentence had already been passed upon his client. Petroc stared after him for a moment, gnawing his lip.

There were paper, quill and ink in the bureau against the wall. He pulled down the flap and sat before it, writing swiftly.

Dear Sir John,

My deepest commiserations upon your present parlous situation. It will be of some comfort to you to learn that your daughter Mistress Dorothy has agreed to become my wife. Her marriage to a citizen whose loyalty to the present government is beyond question will undoubtedly secure her future. I am sure that you appreciate that fact.

> I remain, Sir John,
> Your humble servant,
> Petroc Makin.

It gave him particular pleasure to write that last sentence. He reached for the seal and smiled again, feeling the wax cold and hard in his hand. It was a handsome seal, but he would design a better one for himself.

'I'm ready, but my hair keeps falling down,' Dorothy said plaintively as she came in.

She was in travelling garb, a small box clutched under her arm. Looking at her he felt a moment's tenderness. He would be a good husband and treat her kindly, never reproaching her with her father's treason.

'We'll leave at once,' he said. 'I have taken the liberty of writing to your father to reassure him as to your safety.'

'I thought I heard voices just now.' She looked round innocently.

'I took it upon myself to give orders concerning the carriage, my dear. Shall we leave?'

Solicitously he armed her from the room, ensuring that she was settled comfortably in the carriage before he drew one of the guards aside and gave him the letter.

At the same moment, in the parlour of Ladymoon Manor, Aunt Purity sipped a cup of hot chocolate and motioned to Emma to be seated.

'For I was always averse to getting a stiff neck on account of tilting my head back to see folk,' she said irritably. 'Not that you're so very tall, but it tires me to see you standing there.'

'Then I'll sit, mistress.' Emma took the high-backed chair on the other side of the hearth and folded her hands in her lap.

'You're putting on weight,' Aunt Purity remarked. 'It cannot be pregnancy, so I'd advise you to sample your own cooking less. Mind, there are some men who like a good armful of woman.'

'I'm sure there are.' Emma spoke patiently, knowing that sooner or later the old lady would ramble round to the main subject she had on her mind.

She came to it immediately for once, fixing bright, dark eyes on her house-keeper as she said abruptly.

'He'll wed Dorothy Allston, you know.'

'Who will, mistress?'

'That graceless nephew of mine, of course. It's silly to colour up and shift your gaze, and then pretend not to know what I'm talking about! He's been dangling after her for the last couple of years, and now that Sir John is in prison, he'll likely seize the opportunity to whisk her up the aisle.'

'You do him an injustice,' Emma protested.

'Not I! That nephew of mine will trim his sails to the prevailing wind,' Aunt Purity declared. 'He may look like my brother but there's much in his nature that puts me in mind of my father. When my father made up his mind to do a thing he'd work quietly for its completion. It's that Petroc travels the same road, and that road isn't ended yet.'

'So he will wed Mistress Dorothy, you think? I wish them joy with all my heart,' Emma said.

'You're a good woman,' Aunt Purity said gloomily. 'The good never come off very well, I find. It's a sad state of affairs but I've seen it proved over and over.'

'You don't think very highly of the human race,' Emma reproached.

'I've lived too long to be fooled,' Aunt Purity told her. 'But I think a lot of you, Emma. Always have done, ever since you came to work here as a little lass. You are like your grandmother, Jessie. She was more friend than servant to me, and your grandfather was a fine man. I took an interest in you for their sakes, but now I take an interest in you for your own.'

'You're very kind,' Emma said. Tears had spring into her eyes and she rose, kneeling to mend the fire and blinking hard.

'I was not always kind,' Aunt Purity said. 'I do know, however, what it is to love somebody and lose them. I loved James Rodale even when he went away. I went on loving him, waiting for him to come back to me. Will you go on loving my nephew when he's wed to Dorothy Allston?'

She shot out the last question and Emma flinched as if each word was a little, hard pebble, but she answered serenely, 'Probably I will, but it's up to me to cope with it.'

'Meaning it's none of my business?' Aunt Purity gave an unoffended chuckle.

'I'd not be so rude.' Emma, having mastered her tears, resumed her seat demurely.

'I've altered my will,' Aunt Purity said abruptly.

'I guessed that when you had Master Dalton come over from York while Master Petroc was away.'

'There's not much you miss,' Aunt Purity approved. 'I've left the manor and its contents to my nephew. He's the last of the Makins and he deserves to inherit what Luther would have enjoyed if he hadn't quarrelled with father and run off.'

'Master Petroc has worked very hard,' Emma said.

'Hoping and expecting the place would come to him! Well, I'll not disappoint him. You've not asked what you're getting.'

'I'm waiting to be told,' Emma said calmly.

'I hoped you'd wed, and I could have given you a handsome dowry,' Aunt Purity regretted, 'but I've a feeling you'll never marry. Anyway, whether you do or not, I've left you fifty pounds a year for the rest of your life, and a home here for as long as you choose to stay.'

'That was thoughtful of you,' Emma said.

'There's one thing more, and it's not

in the will. Help me up!' The old lady was struggling to her feet, reaching for the stick she had recently begun to use. 'Come into the Prayer Room, and I'll show you something.'

She led the way into the small room at the back of the hall. It was not a room that was often used, and she entered it with the usual shrinking of her spirits.

'I can always see my father here,' she mused aloud, leaning on her stick and looking about. 'We used to have prayers night and morning, with father thundering hell and damnation at us, and Aunt Hepzibah shivering like a mouse in her corner, and the rest of us crammed in a row. It put me off prayers for life.'

'I've always liked this little room,' Emma said, looking at the dark panelled walls and the circular window above their heads.

'It's very old,' said Aunt Purity. 'I believe that a temple stood here once. The floor is Roman mosaic, undamaged and very beautiful — but my father always said it was too bright and had it covered. I've told you this before, haven't I?'

'Once or twice,' Emma admitted.

'Ah, well, I'm growing old,' Aunt Purity said. 'But there is something you don't know. Pull back the carpet, there's a good lass, and press on the tile beneath. It takes a moment to press on the right place, but one tile slides beneath the other and there's a cavity — ah! now you have it!'

'There's something there.' On her knees Emma peered down.

'Lift it out carefully,' Aunt Purity instructed.

'It's beautiful.' Aware of the inadequacy of her words Emma stared at the golden, twin-handled chalice. A face, engraved on it in silver, gazed back at her. A woman's face, with big slanting eyes and smiling mouth, crowned by a moon from beneath which spirals of silver formed hair.

'It's incredibly old,' Aunt Purity said,

taking it from her. 'The cup was here in Roman times, but it's older than Rome, Greek or Egyptian I think. And used down the centuries, only when it's needed.'

'Needed?'

'There's power here, to be woken into life by the will. For good or evil.' Her old hands gripped the twining snakes that formed the handles, and a shadow fell across her face. 'I'd not have my nephew see this,' she said thoughtfully, 'for fond though I am of him I've a notion he'd not use it aright. You'll keep it hidden when I'm gone.'

'To what end, mistress?'

'Until the one comes who has need of the power and will use it right.'

'I don't understand,' Emma said uneasily.

'No more do I,' said Aunt Purity, 'but my mother was part gypsy, and sometimes the Romany speaks out in me. Put it back now, Emma, and slide back the tile. You'll know when the time to bring it out again has come.'

'I'm sure I hope so,' Emma said doubtfully, replacing it carefully.

'Call it an old woman's whim,' Aunt Purity said wryly. 'I'm past eighty and entitled to whims. But keep the secret, my lass.'

'I promise.'

'And help me back into the parlour. Petroc will be home later with news of the Allstons, I'll wager.'

'I'll see about supper,' Emma began, and was detained by Aunt Purity's hand gripping her sleeve.

'I loved too deeply once,' she said, 'and waited and wasted all my life for him. If the chance to wed comes, then take it. Don't eat out your heart with longing, and then weep when you're old for the years that have fled.'

1726

Interlude

There were times when Dorothy was so unhappy that she wanted to die. On these mornings as soon as she awoke a feeling of hopelessness rushed in upon her, and even if the sun was shining she felt cold and cramped.

'Surely not in the doldrums again, my dear?' Petroc would question in the kind, patient voice that he always used to her. Sometimes she thought she would prefer him to shout at her. Then she would have had some excuse for weeping, but he had never spoken harshly though his every word and gesture reminded her that she was a disappointment to him.

Ten years wed and no living child! Only three miscarriages and a stillborn son had marked the barren years.

'The physician assures me that you are perfectly healthy and could easily carry a child to full term,' Petroc had soothed. 'It has been ill-fortune, nothing more.'

Ill-fortune had dogged her, she thought, ever since her father's execution. After her wedding she had never seen him or heard from him again. She had wanted very much to travel to London for the trial, but it had been impossible for she was already enduring all the discomforts of her first pregnancy.

Petroc had gone down and brought back the news that at the last Sir John had suddenly pleaded guilty, and had willed all his property to King George. Petroc had told her that with a wry smile as if he were laughing at some private jest, but Dorothy, weeping hysterically as she pictured her father lying headless, had paid little attention. And within the day had come the first of the painful, shaming miscarriages that made her feel so wretched.

'If we could go away together,' she had pleaded, 'I'd be so much better.'

But Petroc had embarked on the study of law, and his time was fully occupied. For much of the time he was away from home, in York or London, and when he was at home he locked himself in the larger of the two parlours with massive books and documents spread all about him.

'My education was so scanty that I must begin the study of Latin and Greek from the beginning, so I cannot afford distractions,' he had explained.

That was all very well and she had done her best to understand, but time hung heavily on her own hands. She had never cared much for reading or needlework, and her slight talents at music and drawing were not considered important.

She was even denied the pleasures of conversation for her former friends had speedily faded away upon her father's arrest and, at Ladymoon Manor, there had been only Emma Rowe, who was fully occupied in running the household, and, until her death two summers before, old Aunt Purity who mumbled on and on about people Dorothy had never heard of.

'You should take up riding,' Petroc had advised, 'or go walking. I'm told walking is become a fashionable pastime among the ladies.'

That was no help either. She was terrified of even the gentlest horse, and walking over the rough grass in her high-heeled shoes had resulted in a painfully sprained ankle.

'Today I am thirty-two years' old,' she said aloud, and made a face at her reflection in the glass.

Petroc had been in London for a month but he had given his word that if the case he was prosecuting ended in time he'd come home to celebrate the occasion with her. He was establishing a reputation for himself, she knew, as a quick-witted and ruthless advocate, but it meant he spent even less time with her than before.

Today she was certain however that he would arrive and had dressed with even more than her usual care. Emma, who was clever with a needle, had made the dress of sprigged yellow silk with its green lace bodice and low lace collar. Her brown hair was drawn back into a cluster of ringlets, and her deeply ringed shawl was of a pale spring-green. She had touched her cheeks and lips with rouge, and a diamond sparkled on her finger. Only her eyes bore in their depths a bewildered unhappiness.

'Mistress Dorothy, there's a letter come by the carter, with a parcel attached,' Emma said from the doorway.

Even before she turned from the mirror Dorothy had guessed with a sinking heart, the contents of the letter.

It was as she expected. Petroc was 'too much occupied with pressure of business' to come home for a further week but he sent his love, and he hoped she would enjoy his gift, and he remained her most loving and affectionate husband.

'He is not coming!' she said irritably

to Emma's enquiring look. 'Business is too pressing for him to spare time for his wife's birthday!'

'Ah, now, that's a pity!' Emma exclaimed. 'He'll be sorry not to be here. It must be hard to be a man and tied to a profession.'

'Harder for me, stuck here with nothing to do!' Dorothy snapped, thinking it was just like Emma to take the man's part.

'Indeed it is, mistress,' Emma agreed at once. 'But there's a gift there for you. Why not open it?'

Sulkily she pulled off the wrappings and undid the clasp of the flat case within.

'Pearls, mistress! Oh, but they're lovely!' Emma said.

'Ten of them.' Dorothy fingered the narrow chain. 'One for each year of our marriage.'

'That's a pretty compliment,' Emma said.

'Or a subtle reproach,' Dorothy thought, for pearls were for tears. She wondered if Petroc knew that.

'Will you put them on?' Emma asked.

'Not with this dress. Pearls show up better against a darker shade. Put them away for now.'

'Will you be wanting to eat your birthcake now, or shall we save it for when the master returns?' Emma asked.

'It's my cake,' Dorothy said childishly. 'I shall have a piece tonight after my supper.'

'Very well, mistress.' Emma took up the case and went quietly out.

So it would be supper alone as it so often was. Dorothy sighed, blinking away tears. Outside the parlour windows the sun dappled the lawn, but the room itself was dark with disappointment.

She had never liked Ladymoon Manor. It was a beautiful house, she knew, but she disliked its heavy, dark furnishings, the kitchen which was only a step away from the parlour, the sound of the wind that moaned down the wide chimneys even in the summer, and the stairs and corridors that twisted back upon themselves in a confusing manner.

'It was built from the stones of the nunnery that stood long ago down by the river,' Petroc had told her. 'And long ago a Roman wall had stood here.'

Dorothy had not the faintest interest in Romans but she had heard about nunneries. Nuns were in the habit of dying and coming back to haunt people. It was quite useless for Petroc to assure her that there were no ghosts at Ladymoon Manor. She was convinced that there must be and that it was only a matter of time before she actually saw one.

It was worse since Aunt Purity had died, for apart from a brief visit to London many years before, the old lady had lived all her ninety-two years in the house, and her personality was stamped on every room.

'She loved the house more than anything else in the world,' Petroc had said. 'Oh, she had a love affair — a very brief one, I believe — many years ago, but I don't think any man ever meant so much to her as Ladymoon Manor.'

He had sounded admiring, but Dorothy had privately thought it a terrible way to live. No wonder that Aunt Purity had become a little odd, muttering unintelligently with her skinny fingers fluttering in the air like the skeletons of small birds plucked clean by crows.

'The house won't seem so lonely when our son is born,' Petroc had said in the beginning, and Dorothy had agreed. She had never had anything to do with babies, but it would be agreeable to have one of her own.

And over the years that feeling had become a longing that gnawed at her like hunger. She filled the rooms with imaginary children, a handsome boy who would ride and shoot and stand tall, a girl who would be gentle and pretty, a baby gurgling in a lace-trimmed cradle.

'The babies will come safely when you stop fretting about them,' Petroc had said, and she had heard the conscious patience in his voice and the tiny sigh of relief as he turned back to his books.

The house was suddenly intolerably empty, and at the same time, intolerably confining. She draped the pretty green shawl over her head and went into the hall. Emma was seated in the rocking chair, puffing on the long stemmed clay pipe in which she occasionally indulged. She looked serene and placid, the creaking of the chair the only sound in the big, white-washed apartment.

'I'm going out for a walk,' Dorothy said from the doorway. 'I expect to be an hour or two, but I'll have supper when I return.'

'Yes, mistress,' Emma said. The smoke from her pipe wreathed lazily about her head, and her hands were folded in her lap.

As she went out Dorothy wondered if the housekeeper were ever restless or unhappy. Emma Rowe was not so very much older than she was, but she had no husband or suitor, and though Aunt Purity had left her a handsome annuity she was apparently content to go on working at Ladymoon Manor.

The garden was brilliant with spring. Imperceptibly Dorothy's spirits brightened. It was, after all, foolish to mind so very much that Petroc was not here for her birthday. A birthday was a small matter and Petroc was often away from home. The pearls too had been lovely. She wished they did not remind her so much of tears.

She walked the length of the garden, unlatched the gate and passed through it, raising her skirt as she descended the slope.

Along the river the bushes grew thickly, and flowers speared the long grass that overhung the banks. Deeper in the hollow, at a little distance from the river, trees stood tall and proud, hung with creeper, with here and there a broken piece of masonry.

It was strange, but in this place she felt less lonely than in the house. Perhaps in some way the gentle spirits of the nuns who had once lived in the convent here lingered in the atmosphere, not in a frightening manner but in a fashion that calmed and comforted.

She wandered along the bank, pausing now and then to pick a bloom from those growing so thickly about her. She had always loved flowers, and took pleasure in arranging them, and it was the one gift Petroc had never troubled to bring to her.

Far out from the bank floating on thick stemmed leaves were clusters of golden hearted lily buds. She eyed them longingly, wondering if she might risk stretching for them. It would mean an unpleasant wetting if she slipped, but something in her yearned for the lilies.

'You'll fall in, mistress, if you don't have a care!' a voice from the thicket warned.

Dorothy was so startled that for an instant she almost did fall, tottering on the slippery bank with one hand clutching the air. Two other hands clutched her waist and pulled her back into balance.

'You were not about to damage yourself, I hope? If so, I can give you a push in again,' her rescuer said.

'I was trying to reach the lilies.' She pointed to them, flushing as she met amused black eyes set in a swarthy brown face.

'To finish your bouquet? I'll get them for you.'

The stranger brushed past her and waded into the river. She had scarcely begun to stammer a protest when he clambered back to her, water dripping from his shabby suit, the lilies clutched in his fist.

'You're wet,' she said stupidly.

'I'm used to hardship, and the river is like silk,' he said easily.

'It was very kind of you,' she said.

'The least a gentleman could do! Beautiful ladies ought not to gather their own flowers. Shall we sit among the trees while you weave them into a nosegay?'

She nodded silently, her cheeks still flushed.

'You are right,' he said after a moment as she seated herself on a clump of fern.

'Right?'

'To suspect that I am not a respectable gentleman. Oh, I saw the look in your face, even though you were well-bred enough to try to conceal it, but I'm a rogue and a vagabond, my dear lady!'

'I'm sure I was not thinking any such thing,' Dorothy said primly.

'You're very kind to such a rough and rude fellow,' he said. 'May I sit down?'

'You'll catch cold,' she began, but he was already lowering himself to the grass.

'I've risked worse than a cold in my thirty-five years,' he said easily. 'Ten years back I marched with the Jacobites. Does that shock you?'

She shook her head, confiding, 'My

own father was executed for his own part in the rising.'

'You cannot have been more than a child,' he said with flattering sympathy. 'I hope you didn't suffer too greatly, that people were kind?'

'My husband was — is very good to me,' she said hastily.

'Yet he leaves you to wander about all by yourself and risk drowning for the sake of a few flowers?'

'It's my birthday,' she said shyly. 'I had a fancy for blossom.'

'Then is his offence all the greater! I've a mind to confront him.'

'You've a long walk ahead then,' she said, wanting to laugh. 'He's in London and not home for a week!'

'And I am only here for a week! My caravan is yonder, past the bend in the river.'

'Caravan? Are you a Romany then?'

'My mother always said she was, my father was a Scot though, as pious a hypocrite as you'd hope to meet!'

'And you?'

189

'I'm a travelling physician,' he told her. 'Self-taught.'

'A quack?'

'Hush, dear lady! My feelings are sensitive and easily wounded,' he begged. 'My treatments are very successful, I do assure you, and I compound my own medicines. Doctor Theodore MacWebster, at your service, ma'am.'

He swept a decidedly battered hat from his black head and smiled.

'You were never born with that name!' she exclaimed.

'Not exactly,' he admitted, 'but it looks well, painted across the sides of the caravan. I wish you could see it!'

'Are you offering to escort me there?' she asked.

'It was in my mind, dear lady — no, don't tell me your name! I shall call you Chloe — you look exactly like a Chloe to me. Would you risk your reputation for an hour or two, or are the family likely to come in search of you?'

'Nobody is likely to come in search of

me,' she said, and was only partly aware of the forlornless of her tone.

'Then, if I may be permitted, Mistress Chloe.'

He sprang up and stood before her, still damp and untidy, his eyes twinkling. There was a restlessness about him that made her feel young and gay, as she had not felt for years.

As she held out her hand she thought that Petroc was to be blamed for her indiscretion. It was, after all, her birthday and he had not troubled to come home.

Part Three

1746

1765

8

Tamar was of the opinion that this morning she looked her best. The glass in her room confirmed it, for it reflected a tall, slim young woman whose black hair and eyes contrasted with pale skin and delicate features.

Her hooped gown of white taffeta with its embroidered panels of crimson roses and crystal leaves was a trifle elaborate for morning wear, but she was expecting guests for her birthday dinner and had gone to particular trouble over her toilet.

'Shall I wear powder, Emma?' she asked, frowning at her curled and perfumed head.

'In the middle of the day! I never heard of anything so daft,' Emma said flatly, pinning the crescent-shaped ivory comb to the side of Tamar's head and stepping back to admire the effect.

'They do in London,' Tamar argued.

'Ah, well, there's no accounting for Londoners,' Emma said with a sniff designed to express her opinion of them.

'Do you think I will ever go there?' Tamar asked.

'Your father promised to take you one day,' Emma reminded her.

'Oh, *father*!' Tamar gave a small sniff of her own.

'Father is forever promising to do this or that, but when it comes down to it he's always too busy. Why, he could not even spare the time to come home for my nineteenth birthday!'

'A judge has many claims on his time,' Emma rebuked. 'Your father is an important man, and he does care very deeply for you.'

'I know, I know. I'm the apple of his eye and no other girl in Yorkshire has as many pretty things as I have, or such a beautiful home! Don't scold, darling Emma!'

Tamar rose with the swift grace

characteristic of her and stooped to hug the plump woman whose clear blue eyes and unlined face belied her fifty-odd years. Emma was the only person who ever spoke sharply to her, yet Tamar loved her in many ways even better than her father.

Sir Petroc Makin, recently appointed Judge after a meteoric career as advocate, adored his only child, but being so often absent from home displayed that affection in numerous gifts and a complete inability to say no to anything that Tamar wanted.

Emma, on the other hand, frequently lectured her and had never given her a present in her life, but she was always at home calm and placid and safe. Tamar could dimly recall her mother who had died of the lung-fever when she was five years old. Dorothy Makin had been thin and brown haired with hectic spots of colour in her cheeks, and Tamar had a vague memory of her laughing and of her breaking off to cough.

But for the past fourteen years

Dorothy had lain in the churchyard next to old Aunt Purity and Emma had supplied her place. It was Emma who comforted Tamar when she scraped her knee trying to climb an apple tree, Emma who had accompanied her to York in order to replenish her wardrobe or visit her friends, Emma who had baked cakes and scolded her when her behaviour had sent yet another governess weeping away, Emma who had tucked her in at night and told her stories of the fairies who dwelt in the hollow where a convent had once stood. Emma seemed to have no life of her own outside Ladymoon Manor.

'Did you ever want a family of your own?' Tamar had enquired.

'Why, I have two brothers wed and nieces and nephews,' Emma pointed out.

Tamar made a face. One of Emma's brothers lived up in Scarborough and never came near. The other had married a slattern and begotten a tribe of rough, untidy children who had turned the pleasant house for which Aunt Purity had paid into little better than a hovel.

'I meant a sweetheart,' she said impatiently. 'Did you never fall in love with anybody, Emma?'

'I reckon I did,' Emma said slowly, and for an instant Tamar had glimpsed hunger in her pleasant placid face.

'Why didn't you wed him?'

'Because his fancy never turned to me. He wed someone else.'

'How horrid of him! Why didn't you do the same?'

'Because I never found another to match him,' Emma said.

'So you loved him for ever! That's vastly romantic,' Tamar sighed.

'It's vast nonsense!' Emma said sharply. 'There's nothing romantic about wanting what you can't have!'

'But to be faithful all your life — I think that's beautiful, Emma!'

'A dog does as much,' Emma said wryly.

'I shall be like you,' Tamar was

declaring. 'I shall fall in love and go on loving him for ever, even if he spurns me.'

'Best do some growing up first and then find your man,' Emma advised, and they laughed together though the housekeeper's blue eyes still held a shadow of pain.

Now Emma, tidying scattered pins and ribbons, said, 'Why don't you go downstairs and see that everything is ready for your guests?'

'They'll be here soon.' Tamar gave her reflection a last satisfied glance and went out of the room.

Her bedroom overlooked the garden and, like the sitting room behind it where she had struggled with her lessons under a succession of governesses, was panelled in fashionable walnut, and hung with green and coral. The two apartments on the upper landing housed the occasional guest, and Emma had the two tiny rooms that looked out towards the stables.

Tamar went up the few steps

opposite and opened the door of the master bedroom where her father had slept alone for the past fourteen years. Her mother had died in the tapestry hung bed, but her dresses had long since been given to the poor and her jewels adorned her daughter's person. Poor Dorothy had left as little impression upon this room as she had upon the rest of the house. The great apartment was, like the library, almost aggressively masculine with dark hangings and heavily carved furniture. There were some framed hunting prints in the library, but in the bedroom only one picture decorated the walls.

It was a sombre painting, of grey-green waves lashing a high cliff and above the cliff, glimpsed through swirling cloud a many towered building.

'It reminds me of a house I once saw,' her father had said briefly when she questioned him.

She looked across at the painting wondering why so grim a scene always reminded her of her father who had never raised his voice to her in his life. His walking stick and one of his tricorn hats were laid across the table. Emma was forever tidying them away, but Tamar liked to see them there, for they gave her the illusion that he was at home and likely to walk in at any moment.

Tamar sighed, closing the door gently, and descended the stairs to the hall below. On her left the library doors were open and rows of leather-bound volumes met her gaze.

'I had to educate myself,' her father had said proudly. 'Oh, my mother taught me as much as she could but I was away to sea when I was a lad. That gave me a different kind of education, but when I decided to study the law I had to find tutors in York and London, and learn Latin and Greek.'

Her father's life, Tamar thought, had fallen into three parts. There had been his Cornish childhood when he had grown crops and set lobster pots with his father and listened to his gentle mother as she sang down a moon. Then had come the years at sea when he had known adventure and danger and striven to obtain his master mariner's ticket. And then he had come up into Yorkshire to his father's old home, and brought her mother here and taken up the study and practice of law.

It was a pity she had no close relatives except him. The Makins had died childless, and the Allstons had had only one daughter, Dorothy.

'There are distant cousins of your mother up in Northumbria,' her father had told her. 'Connected with the northern earldoms, but Jacobites all of them!'

The Penhallows were not Jacobites, but equally undesirable for they were fisherfolk and poor farmers, and never paid much heed to him.

'They were only too happy to get my mother married off,' he had said.

The grandmother who had sung down the moon had been lame. Tamar glanced complacently at her own shapely feet and turned towards the parlour. Though it was an unseasonably mild day for January, a fire blazed in the hearth and punch was ready mulled to warm the guests after their jolting ride across the moors.

Three girls with whom she had shared dancing lessons and three young gentlemen, sons of her father's friends, had been invited. They would only stay for the meal and a little gossip before starting for home again, carriage and horses guarded by armed grooms with flaming torches.

'For with the Scots on the march again nowhere is safe,' her father had said. 'Indeed I think it argues much for your popularity, my dear, that your friends will venture out here.'

Ladymoon Manor was very isolated with only the Rowe house a mile distant and a cluster of cottages beyond towards Otley way, but there was little danger of attack. Sir Petroc Makin's reputation was such that it would be a foolhardy rebel who ventured near, and the most they could expect to fear was that some of the sheep would be run off by the army.

Nevertheless the more responsible among the servants had been issued with muskets, and Sir Petroc had instructed his daughter in the use of pistol and rapier.

'You shoot as straight and fence as cleverly as a boy, my love!' he had boasted, and for a fleeting moment it crossed her mind to wonder if he ever regretted that she had not been a son.

His birthday gift to her, a spray of tiny rubies set in gold lay in its velvet lined box on the parlour table. She pinned it to the shoulder of her dress and took up the ivory fan that had been his Christmas present. He had not been home for that festival either.

At the other side of the main hall the finishing touches were being put to the dinner. The dais with its white covered table and high-backed chairs and sparkling crystal was curtained off from the huge, white-washed kitchen, and a bowl of snowdrops stood by her plate.

There would be salmon trout, and duckling in cream, venison in a red wine sauce, rabbit and chicken pies, pease-pudding and mushrooms stuffed with ginger, candied fruit and blackberry preserve pie. The punch was warmed and the wines chilled, and on the iced cake in the middle of the table her name was picked out in little silver balls.

There was the jangling of harness beyond the front door and in sudden anticipation she hastened to open it, in time to see two riders in greatcoats descending with much stamping of feet and flapping of arms.

'Don't pretend you're frozen, William Marsh,' she called scornfully from the doorway, 'for this is the warmest January we've had for years!'

'Greetings, Mistress Tamar!' The young man strode up the steps and kissed her hand. 'I behave like this in order to make my companion feel at home, for he is from the south and feels every gust of wind!'

'Oh?' She looked enquiringly at the tall figure behind him.

'Sir Taverne Bostock is on a visit from Cornwall,' William said. 'I took the liberty of bringing him with me in the hope you won't object to an extra guest.'

'I welcome him,' she said promptly. 'But where are the others?'

'Twenty minutes' ride away. The axle broke and the wheel is split, so the coach cannot proceed. Can you send grooms back with me to repair it?'

'Take whoever and whatever you need. Is anyone hurt?'

'The young ladies had a slight shaking but are more anxious for the state of their pretty clothes,' William assured her. 'I'll ride back with the grooms to show them where we're stranded. Taverne, will you stay and entertain Mistress Tamar? 'Tis the least we can offer her if the dinner is to be delayed.'

'Come in, Sir Taverne.' She drew her

skirt aside to let him pass. 'Will you have some punch, William, before you start back?'

'I'd best see your grooms, and make sure they have a wheel. We didn't carry a spare.'

He was remounting, his face slightly flushed with importance. For all his good humour William thrived on the occasional disaster. It was also typical of him to bring an extra guest at the last minute.

Emma, in her best grey silk, bustled through from the parlour.

'Dinner will have to be put back, Emma,' Tamar said. 'There's a wheel come off the coach but nobody is hurt and William is riding back with the men and we have an extra gentleman for the meal.'

'Sir Taverne Bostock, ma'am.' Recognising Emma's status he bowed, hat in hand. 'I am staying here in York at the moment and Master Marshall was kind enough to ask me to accompany him and your other guests.

I hope it does not inconvenience you too greatly.'

'We can set an extra place,' Emma said cordially. 'Tamar, take your guest into the parlour and offer him some punch. I'll have cook to see to the dinner lest the pies scorch.'

'If you'll come this way, sir.' The flurry of the moment over, she preceded him into the other room.

'This is most hospitable of you, Mistress Makin,' the visitor said. 'I am a newcomer in the north, but already I have learned that the people are most kind.'

'We do try to make folk welcome. Let me take your coat, and come to the fire if you're feeling the cold.'

'William was teasing,' he said, shrugging off the many caped garment. 'We are not all weaklings in Cornwall, I do assure you.'

'I'm quite sure of that.' She offered him punch. 'My own father was born and reared there.'

'So William mentioned to me. The

name was not familiar to me, but my parents spent much of their time abroad in the years before my father's death, and I travelled with them. Your health, Mistress Makin.'

'Tamar.' She took the chair opposite him and raised her glass.

'An unusual name.'

'It's from the Bible, I think.'

'It's also the name of a river. Your father must have a great affection for his native county.'

'He hasn't been back there for years. He made his life up here in the north,' she informed him.

'And in a beautiful house. It is smaller than Bostock Towers, but the atmosphere here is so warm and pleasant. Has the house been long in your family?'

'My grandfather bought it. I don't know exactly who lived here before that. An old half-crazy woman, I believe. I've lived here all my life.'

'And today is your birthday. I took the liberty of bringing a small gift.'

'Oh, but that was most thoughtful of you, sir!'

She accepted the parcel with pleasure and tore at the wrappings with the impulsive eagerness that made her seem younger than she was.

'A hand mirror, and so prettily embossed.'

'I found it in a shop in York and thought it a charming trifle,' he said, 'but now that we have met I make bold to say that when you look into it then it becomes truly exquisite.'

'Why, thank you, sir!' She lowered the mirror and stared at him in confusion.

The young gentlemen of her acquaintance were not given to subtle compliments, but this black-haired stranger had the air of a sophisticate. He was, she judged, looking at him with closer attention, older than most of her friends, being already in his thirties, with lines of experience furrowing his lean cheeks. His eyes were as dark as her own, and he had raised them to her face with a searching glance that brought the colour back into her cheeks.

'Do you think you will know me when we meet again?' he enquired gently.

'Why, yes, no — you muddle me, sir.' She waved her fan energetically, 'I am not accustomed to your Cornish humour.'

'Nor I to Yorkshire modesty. We shall have to grow accustomed to each other, ma'am.'

'You will not be leaving York soon then?' she said breathlessly.

'I hope to spend several months here,' he told her. 'I've spent so long on the Continent that I have had no leisure to explore the beauties of my own land. Perhaps, if your father permits it, we could explore the countryside together on occasion. You do ride?'

'As well as I walk,' she assured him.

'Then you must be a superb rider.' He raised the glass and drank to her again, his black eyes admiring.

'Tell me about Cornwall,' she invited. 'My father left the district when he was a lad and speaks little of it.'

'There are quiet coves,' he said slowly, 'and jagged rocks that stick up like teeth. But the climate is very mild. We have blossom in winter there and never see snow. Our moors are not as vast as yours and of gentler aspect. The mist hangs heavily upon them, and it's said to this day, if you listen carefully, you can still hear the Roman legions marching.'

'And your home is large?'

'A stark, clifftop castle, many towered, with high walls all about it. I grew up there, so it never seemed strange to me.'

'I would like to see it all,' she said eagerly. 'My father is always promising to take me to London but it never comes to anything, and he will be more occupied than ever now that he is made Judge.'

'You would like Cornwall much

better than London,' he assured her. 'The city gets dirtier every year, and the Court is full of Germans.'

'That is exactly what I keep telling her, sir,' Emma said, coming in. 'Far better for folk to stay at home.'

'Much you know of it! You've never been further than Otley in your life,' Tamar said crossly. 'Sir Taverne, this is Emma Rowe, who is the real mistress of Ladymoon Manor, though it amuses her to pretend she is the housekeeper.'

'I beg pardon, ma'am, but I took you for the governess,' he bowed.

'Lord, no! I frightened all my governesses away when I was young and wild,' Tamar exclaimed.

'And time hasn't improved your disposition,' Emma said dryly. 'You've a smut on your nose, Missy.'

'A smut? I'll tidy myself before the others get here!' Snatching up the hand mirror, she whisked out of the room.

'She's an enchanting creature,' Sir

214

Taverne observed, staring after her.

'Her father sets more store by her than by anything else in the world,' Emma said.

She had taken Tamar's vacated seat and her voice held a faint note of warning.

'Then he is very wise not to expose her to the corruptions of London life,' he returned equally. 'I would think more than twice before I took a daughter of mine there.'

'You have daughters, sir?'

'Neither daughters nor wife, ma'am. I am a lonesome bachelor.'

'Are there no young ladies in the south?'

'Very many,' he assured her, 'but flowers from a different garden often smell sweeter.'

'Aye, well this particular flower is not for the picking,' Emma said, 'unless you intend to bind it with a marriage knot, of course.'

'I take your meaning.' He inclined his dark head towards her. 'Mistress

Tamar is not, I hope, already promised?'

'Not yet, sir.'

'Then there would be no objection to my calling upon her? With her father away from home — '

'He relies on my discretion, sir, as to how much freedom to allow her.'

'But you would permit me to call upon her — as a friend?'

'Indeed I would, sir, and I know I can speak for her father in that,' Emma said. 'He'll not be home for more than a month, but if you stay that long he will be happy to meet you, I'm sure. He was born and reared in Cornwall.'

'So William Marshall told me, but the name was not a familiar one.'

'His mother had the name of Goda Penhallow.'

'Now that's a common name round us!' he exclaimed. 'There are many Penhallows in Cornwall. But I hope to spend several months in the north.'

'And will be most welcome,' said Emma.

'If Emma says that you may be sure you're in high favour,' Tamar said, returning. 'She is a veritable dragon, I do assure you.'

'I hear the other guests coming,' Emma warned her. 'Others? Oh, yes, of course!' She had forgotten the other guests and experienced a momentary irritation at their having arrived. It would have been so agreeable to have eaten a meal with Sir Taverne Bostock as her sole companion.

'Shall we go and greet them, mistress?' Sir Taverne enquired.

'Yes, indeed!' She laid her hand on his sleeve with a little proprietary gesture.

They matched well together, Emma thought with unwonted indulgence. Both were tall and dark, the girl's fragile complexion and beautiful gown contrasting with her companion's more swarthy aspect and nutbrown clothes.

The girl would have to wed sooner or later, and Emma was of the opinion that the best husband would be an older man to spoil her as her father did and curb the streaks of wildness in her nature.

9

Sir Petroc Makin took off his curled white wig and ran his fingers through his cropped hair. It had been a long tiring day and the Courts had stank even more foully than usual. The city itself stank, thick smoke belching from every chimney, the gutters piled with rotting refuse. It was little wonder that disease was rampant or that those who could afford it avoided the narrow streets and built their houses in airy squares away from the congestion of the alleys.

His own apartments were just off Lincoln's Inn Fields. He had maintained them over several years and would not have been comfortable in more luxurious surroundings, though he assumed his recent elevation meant he would be expected to move to larger premises.

But his parlour, with bedroom leading off it, and a small drawing room beyond suited him. Leather made the couch and chairs slippery, and the oak panelled walls were bare of ornament. Heavy curtains shut out the swirling snow that whitened the view, and a fire roared in the hearth. Books and papers were piled on the tables, and a decanter of brandy stood near his elbow.

He set the wig on its stand and poured himself a drink. Only a few more days and he would brave the roads back to Yorkshire. The unseasonably mild weather had broken and frost rimed the panes and made slush of the muddy streets.

It would be good to be back in Ladymoon Manor. Good to walk through the garden down to the river, or sit in the enormous library with his books around him, the smell of baking drifting through the kitchen, his daughter telling him of her latest jaunt to York.

Those who had only seen Sir Petroc

Makin arguing a case in Court or instructing a clerk would not have recognised the gentleness of his expression as his mind turned to his daughter. She was the one thing in his life that mattered more than his house or the legal profession to which he had devoted nearly thirty years.

Tamar was, he thought, very beautiful, so beautiful that he sometimes caught his breath as he looked at her. Emma had reared her well after her mother's death. The child was growing into an exquisite young woman.

He sighed, knowing that before long he would have to arrange a suitable marriage for her. He would make certain that the man loved her truly and treated her kindly, and he hoped very much that they would continue to make their home at Ladymoon Manor. He could not have borne to see her leave.

'Excuse me, Sir Petroc.' His manservant had tapped twice on the parlour door before he had roused from his abstraction.

'I thought I said I didn't require anything more this evening,' he said irritably.

'I know, sir, but a lady wishes to see you.'

'Has she an appointment?'

The man shook his head.

'Then get her to make one and to see me in Chambers.'

'She says it is a personal matter of the utmost importance.'

'And does she have a name, this importunate lady?'

'Bostock. Lady Catriona Bostock,' the man said.

The name he had neither spoken nor heard for more than thirty years hit him like a bullet. He shook his head slightly, hearing the echo of the word like a roaring in his ears.

'Shall I let her up, sir?'

'Yes, yes. Show her up.' He reached for his wig and put it on carefully, his fingers trembling a little.

The woman who came in was the girl he had known grown old. As she removed her mantle, dropping it over the servant's outstretched arm, he had a flash of her standing tall and proud on the staircase. Her figure in its wide, panniered skirts had retained its elegance, and under the white wig her face had the same taut, beautiful bones though her eyes were sunken, her small mouth painted.

'Lady Bostock? Won't you sit down? You'll take some refreshment on this inhospitable evening?'

He had regained command of himself but she shook her head, motioning the manservant to leave and taking a chair at some distance from the fire.

'You are a Judge now, I believe?' Her voice was cool, a faint edge of amusement apparent.

'Recently appointed,' he said curtly. 'Are you here to congratulate me?'

'No, on more urgent business.'

She drew off long silk gloves and flexed her fingers slightly. He saw then that the joints were enlarged and shiny.

'Rheumatics,' she said, seeing his

glance. 'Infirmity attacks us all.'

'I am sorry,' he said.

'It's of little consequence.' She lifted her shoulders in a little, foreign gesture. 'It is not the ache in my bones that brings me to you.'

'You're very welcome,' he said, forcing geniality into his voice.

It was shaming but after all these years her mere presence rendered him inadequate, a stumbling lad in awe of his betters.

'Neither am I here for a social visit,' she said. 'It gives me no pleasure to see you again.'

'It was a long time ago,' he said uneasily.

'I despised you for it,' Catriona said. 'I hated and loathed you for forcing me.'

'And now?'

'Now I care nothing about you at all,' she said coldly. 'Oh, I've heard of your career from various sources. I made it my business to do that.'

'Hoping I would fail?'

'Fearing you would succeed, and it seems my fears were justified. You have risen high, and proved my opinion of your ability wrong.'

He inclined his head.

'But not my opinion of your character,' she said quickly. 'You were never a gentleman, Sir Petroc Makin. I can only hope that you did not mistreat your wife as you mistreated me. She died some years ago, I understand?'

He nodded silently.

'My own husband died three years ago,' she said. 'Ours was not a happy union.'

'I am sorry for it,' he said.

'Jeremy was a weak, foolish man,' Catriona said. 'He was more interested in his luck at the gaming tables than in his marriage, but I must give him credit for never revealing that our son was not, in fact, his.'

'Son? You bore a son?'

'Your son,' Catriona said, and there was a dismal triumph in her voice and face. 'I bore your son.'

'You cannot be certain,' he said at last.

'Oh, but I can be.' Her tone was light and bitter. 'Jeremy was an unsatisfactory husband in many ways, including the most important one. Our marriage was never fully consummated.'

'A son.' He echoed her words blankly.

'I told him there had been a — liaison with a man who had since died. He was kind, partly out of guilt, I suppose. He even grew very fond of the child.'

'Child? He must be a man grown by now,' Petroc said slowly.

'Older than you were when you dishonoured me,' she said. 'I named him Taverne after my father, the only real man I ever knew.'

'A son. I am — to be told this after so many years!' He stared at her. 'But why do you come now?'

'You married a woman called Dorothy Allston,' she said, 'whose father was beheaded for his part in the Fifteen rebellion.'

'Yes.'

'And you have a daughter? A girl named Tamar?'

'She knows nothing of you or of Bostock Towers.'

'You are very fond of your daughter, I believe?'

'She means everything to me,' he said.

'As my son does to me. We should keep in closer touch with our children.'

'I don't follow,' he said in bewilderment.

'You have been away from home for some time, I take it.'

'Since before Christmas, but I return at the end of the week.'

'You have received no letters from her?'

'Tamar hates writing letters. She is a very active, energetic girl.'

'My son also seldom writes letters,' Catriona said. 'However he did write to me recently, telling me that he has

227

travelled up into Yorkshire and has met the lady to whom he intends to offer marriage. Must I spell out her name?'

Blood drummed in his temples and the room swam before him. From a great distance he heard Catriona say mockingly,

'So you are not entirely without feelings? You do care about your daughter.'

'Goddam it! Of course I care!' He was blinking rapidly, forcing the dizziness to recede.

'You understand why I have come?' For the first time her voice had softened and there was pleading in her dark eyes. 'It cannot be permitted. Such an alliance would be — '

'Unclean,' he said harshly. 'It would be — I have not the words.'

'You will have to prevent it,' she said flatly. 'I travelled from Cornwall as soon as Taverne's letter reached me. There is nothing I can do, for he is a man grown. But your daughter is under age?'

'Nineteen.' He rose and paced to the window, drawing aside the heavy curtain to peer out at the drifting. 'She is scarce nineteen.'

'Young enough to get over her disappointment. Taverne will fare worse. He has had the usual amorous adventures, but this is the first time he has been set on marriage.'

'I wanted her to be happy,' Petroc said in a low voice. 'Dorothy and I were wed for eleven years before she produced a living child, and after Tamar there were no others. I have spoiled her a little perhaps, but she is sweet and wild and I wanted her to be happy, to marry a man for whom she has a real affection.'

'From what Taverne says in his letter she has a 'real affection' for her own half-brother,' Catriona said.

'To let him go into Yorkshire!' He swung round from the window and stared at her accusingly. 'Might you not have prevented it?'

'I told you he's a man grown. He

comes and goes as he pleases. It was merely Providence that he wrote to me now before he asked for your daughter's hand.'

'Is he like me?' Petroc asked.

'He resembles my father,' she said briefly. 'At least I was spared having to watch him grow up looking like you.'

'Tamar is not like me either,' he said. 'She's dark as a gypsy but much prettier than any Romany I ever saw. Sometimes — sometimes I've fancied that she looks like the daughter you and I might have had.'

'When I knew I was with child,' she said, 'I tried to get rid of it. I tried every way that I knew, but the babe was determined to be born. And Jeremy was kind. He accepted the boy as his own and grew to love him as I did.'

'We are talking in circles,' Petroc said. 'We could go on and on and get nowhere at all. The fact remains that our son wishes to marry my daughter and we can neither of us contemplate such a thing.'

'It's for you to forbid it,' Catriona said, beginning to rise. 'It was your fault in the beginning.'

'After you had cheated me and driven my mother out of her home?' The colour mounted in his broad face. 'I trusted you and loved you — yes, *loved!* I went away to make myself worthy of you. That's the truth. But to you I was a lout, a peasant! You cared nothing for me, nothing for anyone except yourself. But in the end I took you.'

'Took me, yes.' She stood very still for a moment, her head raised, her face still beautiful in the candlelight. 'But you never possessed me. You never possessed me for one single second!'

He thought he'd put out his hand towards her, but she had gone before he could frame any words and he was staring across an empty room at the closed door.

He had not enquired where she was staying nor how she had learned his whereabouts. He had not even insisted on giving her some refreshment. There were other questions that rose up now, tormenting him. Had she never, in all the long years, regretted her actions? Had she truly driven all desire out of her heart?

They were useless questions and he was only filling his mind with them because he could not yet endure the other questions that were forcing themselves into consciousness.

If his son — dear God, but how he had wanted a son! — if Taverne Bostock had fallen in love with Tamar, it was possible they had already made love. His fists clenched as he contemplated that possibility. Tamar was a good girl and Emma guarded her jealously, but if Taverne Bostock were — he would go insane if he allowed such imaginings to crowd into his mind.

Returning to the fire he gulped down some brandy, waiting until his hands no longer trembled. Then he opened the door and shouted for his manservant.

The state of the roads was not important. What mattered was that he should reach home as soon as possible and put an end to the wretched, unspeakable affair.

At Ladymoon Manor Emma said sternly to her charge, 'You must write to your father and tell him of this matter if he does not arrive in the next few days. It is most undutiful of you not to inform him.'

'I hate writing letters,' Tamar said impatiently. 'And this isn't something to be put down in a letter. I want to tell him all about it myself.'

'Well, I'm sure I hope it's the right thing to do,' Emma said doubtfully. 'I'd have liked it better if Sir Petroc had met the gentleman.'

'He will meet him, just as soon as he comes home. Taverne is going to ride over every morning, to see if father has arrived.'

'That won't be unusual. He's been here nearly every day for the past month,' Emma said dryly. 'It's a wonder he's not worn himself clean out, riding up and down from York as often as he does.'

'Taverne's very strong. He's used to travelling all over for long distances,' Tamar said proudly.

'But he ought to have spoken to your father first,' Emma fretted.

'Oh, he wouldn't have said anything to me,' Tamar assured her, 'but I teased it out of him. I told him I feared I would soon be on the shelf if I didn't make up my mind to a husband, and I hinted that I was very fond of William Marshall.'

'Tamar!' Emma sounded shocked but her mouth was curving into a reluctant smile.

'He looked quite fierce when I said that. You've no idea how black he can look when he's angry! And he gripped my hand so tightly that I almost cried out and he said, 'Mistress, as soon as your father returns it's my intention to speak to him, to offer for your hand'. That was what he said, Emma. I was

234

too excited to speak, and then he said, 'I've written to my mother and told her that I've found the girl I want to wed. Will you say the same to your father?' '

'And did you speak then?'

'I said — I said that I loved him, and that I would never love any other man.' Tamar hesitated, twisting her fingers together, and burst out, 'Was it wrong of me, Emma? Was it wrong to admit as much when he hasn't met my father yet? I wanted him to know, to be sure of me. Was that wrong of me, Emma?'

'I reckon not,' Emma said slowly.

'We'll live here for most of the time,' Tamar said.

'But we'll go to Cornwall too. Bostock Towers stands on a high cliff, overlooking a little cove with the sea rushing in over the needle rocks. They have moors there too. Taverne says, gentler ones than ours. And there's a river called the Tamar. I must ask father if I was named after the river!'

'Cornwall sounds interesting,' Emma said.

'You must come with us when we travel south,' Tamar said, slipping from her seat and sitting on the carpet at Emma's knee. 'You've never travelled any place, at all, have you?'

'And I'm too old to start travelling now,' Emma said. 'Who'd take care of your father if I were to go travelling?'

'He's mainly away in London, anyway,' said Tamar. 'And he'll probably come to Cornwall with us, to meet Lady Bostock. It's too far I suppose for her to travel for the wedding. She has rheumatism, Taverne says. But she was very beautiful when she was young. She has Spanish blood, Taverne says, and is very elegant and proud. Do you think she will approve of me, as a wife for Taverne?'

'Happen she will, if you don't chatter too much,' Emma said. 'It's all come about so fast. That's what frets me.'

'The best things happen quickly,' Tamar said, her face glowing in the firelight.

'Aye, perhaps they do.'

It had happened quickly to her, she thought. The coming through the orchard into the garden and seeing the tall gentleman with the sun bleached hair. She had known then, in that second, that her life would never be quite the same again.

There had even been a little while when she had hoped he might wed her, but it had only been a dream. Petroc was too ambitious to content himself with a servant girl. And by the time Dorothy had died it was too late, for he had achieved everything he wanted, and Emma in his eyes had never been more than a trusted servant.

'I shall never love anyone else as long as I live!' Tamar was declaring. 'I shall be like Aunt Purity, but my story will have a happy ending.'

'I'm sure I hope so,' Emma said, hiding the gentleness of her wishing in sour words. 'But you'd best not count your chickens before they peck their way out of the eggs. A little caution never hurt anybody.'

'Pooh! Who cares for caution!' Tamar gave the housekeeper a quick, fierce hug and scrambled to her feet. 'I shall go to bed,' she informed her, 'and dream of Cornish moors and a lady with Spanish blood and of loving the same man for ever and ever! Good-night!'

Her going left the parlour a lonelier place. It was past nine o'clock and the other servants were abed, the three maids in the loft over the back scullery, Cook in privileged privacy next to the stillroom, the men over the stables. The fires in the kitchen had been banked and the floor and tables scrubbed down. The doors were bolted and the windows shuttered against the wind and snow. The roads would be treacherous but there was no point in worrying. Sir Petroc had come home in worse weather. It would have been pleasant, Emma thought, to have had a dog, to sit with her in the nights when sleep came hard, but for some reason Petroc disliked them. The men used a couple to herd the sheep and fox-hounds for hunting were kennelled at Otley, but he had never allowed a house dog, though several cats had taken up residence in the stables.

The fire would keep in until morning. She gave it a cursory glance and took up her candle. Across the side hall the library was in darkness but a solitary light burned at the foot of the stairs. Tamar would be in bed by now, her clothes flung carelessly about, her eyes closed, for she fell asleep as effortlessly as a healthy young animal.

'She is like my own child,' Emma thought, and remembered the long nights when she had lain wakeful in her small bedroom and tried not to imagine what was happening behind the closed door of the master bedroom where Dorothy and Petroc shared the big tester bed. Even after Dorothy had died Emma had still lain awake listening for footsteps across the landing, thinking, 'He and I are not so old, and all men have needs'. But he had never come, had never asked for anything save that she rear his child and keep his household running smoothly during his frequent absences.

She went up the wide staircase, hesitated on the landing where an old spinning wheel stood, and then turned, not towards her own bedroom but in the direction of the master bedroom. Once inside, she set her candle on the dresser, slid the bolt across the door, and lit three further candles. The edges of the room were still in darkness but radiance spread over the dark counterpane, the table on which a spare pair of his reading spectacles were placed.

This was her own rare and private pleasure, to be indulged only when there was no possibility of her being interrupted. Slowly she drew off her shoes, wriggling her toes with relief as the constricting leather was removed. Raising her arms she took off the lace-trimmed cap and shook down her hair. It was still thick and soft, retaining much of the colour. She twined her fingers through it, letting the slight headache that often afflicted her at the end of a long day, drain away.

Under her the bed was soft and comforting. She lay still, her eyes half-closed, while the play in her mind rolled past.

'You're late tonight, Petroc. Did you have a good day?'

'Tiring. It's good to be with you, my lovely Emma.' His imagined body lay lean and hard against her. His imagined hands drew her bodice from her shoulders, stroked her breasts, her arms, her thighs. She shivered, waiting for the curtain to descend upon the final act.

'I have always loved you, Emma. There never was a woman like you.'

'There's no secret in it. I happen to love you, that's all.'

His imagined mouth pressed her lips into silence, and the curtain came down.

It was cold and she guessed that the snow was falling faster. She rose, smoothing the quilt, snuffing out the candles except her own. Then, with her cap and shoes wedged under her arm, she opened the door and padded to her room, her shadow bobbing ahead of her on the wall.

10

'It is, I know, impossible but every time I see you you have grown more lovely since the last time we met!' Taverne exclaimed.

'Why, thank you, sir! Will you say the same I wonder after we have been wed for a year?'

'I will say the same when we have been wed for twenty years!'

'Lord, but I shall be nearly forty!' Tamar cried. 'How shall I endure that?'

'By lying about it, as other ladies do,' he said.

'Fie on you! What a shocking slander!' She swung away from him in a flurry of pink and blue velvet, her face a mixture of offence and amusement.

'My love, I never tell lies about ladies,' he said solemnly. 'They do it so beautifully for themselves.'

'I swear I'll not listen,' she declared. 'Emma, tell him to behave himself!'

'I hear the coach,' Emma said. On her face was the look of strained excitement that Tamar had noticed before when Sir Petroc was expected.

'You don't have to worry. He'll not be screaming for an instant dinner,' she said. 'Oh, Taverne, now you will meet him at last! I know you'll like him, and I know that he will approve of you! Emma, where is my cloak? I must run and greet him!'

'In those slippers, in that snow! You'll stay right here, missy,' Emma said firmly, bustling to the door herself.

As always the housekeeper was filled with conflicting emotions. Joy at having Petroc home again was restrained by the control she placed upon herself.

'Good afternoon, sir.' She dropped a neat curtsy, her plump hands tightly clasped. 'Did you have a hard journey? We were afraid the roads might be too bad.'

'It took longer than usual, but we

stopped over at some very admirable inns.'

'But you'll be glad of your own bed again, I daresay.' She nodded cordially past him to where Bob, his man-servant, was struggling with the luggage.

'Hang up my cloak, there's a good girl!' He tossed it to a maid hovering in the kitchen doorway.

'Where is Tamar? I thought I glimpsed her at the parlour window a moment since.'

'She is — she is entertaining a friend,' Emma said, hoping that the bad temper occasioned, she supposed, by the rigours of his journey, would not endure past his first glass of madeira.

'In here, father! Do come!' Tamar's voice sounded higher and breathless as if a sudden fit of apprehension had seized her.

Petroc went by Emma into the parlour and stopped, shaking snow from his boots, frowning across to where they stood side by side, hands lightly touching.

Though it was scarcely past midday the dull skies had made candles necessary, and in the blaze of light from them both Taverne and Tamar looked, for an instant, as unreal as two characters in a play.

Then Tamar came and flung her arms round him as if she were still a child. But she was a young woman. Her high breasts and the awakened look in her dark eyes told him that, and he felt a sick anger at what had to be done.

'Father, I would like to present Sir Taverne Bostock,' she said. 'He is from Cornwall, from your own part of the country. Taverne, this is my father who is newly appointed a Judge!'

He hadn't wanted to look closely at the man but the figure in blue satin was bowing before him and he heard his own voice, stiff with fear and disapproval.

'I was not aware my daughter had guests, sir. You must pardon my own attire but I am just returned after a long journey, and have not yet changed.'

'Taverne has been here every day in hope of your arrival,' Tamar said. 'He has ridden up and down from York despite the snow. I told him it would be more sensible of him to stay over, but Emma said it would not be proper.'

'Emma was quite right,' Petroc said shortly.

Catriona had spoken the truth in saying that her son did not resemble him. He was dark-haired, hawk-nosed, like the older Sir Taverne with whom he had struck the bargain so long ago. Yet he thought too that he could detect something of himself in the way the young man held his head.

'Riding is no hardship to me, sir,' Taverne was saying. 'Mistress Tamar and I were introduced by a mutual friend. I knew William Marshall years since at school, and when I made up my mind to come into Yorkshire, I wrote to him of my intention.'

'Why did you come into Yorkshire in the first place?' Sir Petroc asked, accepting a glass of madeira from Emma and motioning her to leave in so brusque a manner that colour flamed in her cheeks.

'I've spent many years abroad,' Taverne said. 'My own land has charms I've not yet explored.'

'It's women too, I daresay.'

'Father!' Tamar's voice was so full of hurt that he winced.

'I met your daughter by chance, not design,' Taverne said.

'And have been back every day since. So Tamar has said.'

'In the hope of seeing you, Sir Petroc.'

'On business?'

'In a manner of speaking, but I would regard it more as a personal matter.'

'He wants to wed me,' Tamar interrupted. 'He wishes to offer for me, father, so you must stop glaring at him as if you were in the Courts, and take him by the hand like a friend!'

It was out, and the worst part was still to come.

'Your father is weary,' Taverne said. 'You should not have blurted it so impetuously, my love.'

'Tamar, go to your room,' her father said.

'But I want to stay here,' she began.

'To your room,' he repeated, so harshly that tears started to her eyes. 'You will stay there until you are called. Sir Taverne, we'd better go into my library where we can be more private.'

'Don't be angry,' Tamar said, and at a look from her suitor broke off, looked miserably from one to the other, and rustled from the room.

'This has been a shock for you,' Taverne said, 'and I blundered in rushing my fences, but it has been almost as great a shock to me. I never expected to have my heart captured so completely.'

Sir Petroc, ignoring him, strode through into the library and stood, near the flat-topped table on which books and documents were neatly stacked. He was breathing heavily, the pulse at his temple beating hard. God in Heaven, but the lad was like him whatever Catriona might think. Oh, not in feature or colouring but in several subtle, indefinite mannerisms. Here was the son he'd always wanted, and now could never claim.

'Sir Petroc.' Taverne had followed him and carefully shut the door.

'Well, what of this nonsense?' the older man demanded.

'Not nonsense, sir, though we chose the time badly. I wish to marry Mistress Tamar. That's a rough way to put it, but we can discuss the matter fully when you're rested!'

'There's nothing to discuss,' Sir Petroc said.

'Sir, with respect, I think there is. I love your daughter and wish to make her my wife. There are many questions you will want to ask me. I respect that! Tamar is still very young and has seen nothing of the world and you know nothing of me. All that can be resolved.'

'There is nothing to resolve. The

matter is closed.'

But looking at his son's darkening face, he knew with a sinking heart that a flat refusal would not suffice.

'A gentleman whose honourable proposal is refused has the right to ask for reasons, Sir Petroc. I demand that right.'

'This is my house — and your demands are impertinent.'

'Nevertheless I make them,' Taverne said. 'I am of an ancient Cornish family, Sir Petroc, and my house and estate is a large and a prosperous one. Tamar will want for nothing.'

'She wants for nothing here.'

'Save a husband, sir. A loving husband.'

'She has a loving father.'

'I have a loving mother, sir, but it is not at all the same thing.'

He was right of course. Tamar ought to be wed and bear children. This man, were he anyone else's son, would have been the husband he would have chosen.

'We would both be willing to wait,' Taverne was continuing. 'I'm aware it's a very short time since we met and you have had no opportunity of forming any estimate of my character. Tamar is young and we wish to marry with your blessing.'

'You have it not, and never will have!'

'Then you must give me your reason, sir, else when she comes of age we will be compelled to wed without it.'

'Tamar cannot wed,' Sir Petroc said. 'She cannot wed anybody.'

'But why? There has to be a reason!'

'Not one I care to discuss.'

Even now he might not be forced to this monstrous lie.

'Then when she is of age I shall wed her without blessing, and so I give you fair warning.'

'My daughter cannot wed,' Sir Petroc said, 'because she is not fit for it.'

'Not fit?' Taverne knit black brows, staring at him.

'Her mother, Dorothy Allston, was — she was a delicate, highly-strung creature. I wed her after her father had been arrested so I had no opportunity of speaking to him, of finding out more about her. We lost several babes before she bore Tamar, and I prayed the joy of motherhood would cure her.'

'Cure her of what?'

'Her wits were disordered,' Sir Petroc said, looking down at the table. 'Oh, it was not apparent on the surface. There were months when she was completely lucid. But she ought never to have been married. An eminent physician whom I consulted told me that the condition was inherited. Had Dorothy remained spinster, dwelling quietly at home, the mania would have lain dormant. Marriage and the bearing of children wakened it into life. She died practically imbecile when Tamar was five.'

He forced himself to raise his eyes, to meet the other's stricken gaze.

'Tamar is not her mother,' Taverne said at last. 'It's possible she could marry without hurt.'

'Possible, but would it be fair to

subject her to such a terrible risk? She is like her mother in temperament already.'

'Other physicians? There are doctors on the Continent — '

'Who would tell you the same thing.'

'Lord God!' Taverne had sunk down to a chair. 'She is so lovely,' he said hopelessly. 'So full of life and to have this dreadful shadow hanging over her.'

'She knows nothing of it. I will try to keep the knowledge from her for as long as I possibly can.'

'A heavy burden for you too, sir. I never guessed — ' His voice trailed away and he made a helpless gesture with his hands.

'I am truly sorry,' Sir Petroc thought. 'Sorry to have forced a proud woman against her will, to have begotten a son whom I can never claim, to have slandered a poor, dead wife who did me no harm.'

'I had best leave,' Taverne said. 'I had best ride away at once.'

'If there was even the possibility of

hope I would have told you so,' Sir Petroc said.

'And you are like the lad I used to be, my son. Having no guile yourself you did not suspect it in others.'

'I wish — I wish I had never come into Yorkshire,' Taverne said.

He had risen, and was obviously composing himself into a semblance of calm. After a few moments he bowed and went out again, closing the door with a soft finality.

It was over. He had met his son, had prevented an unlawful and unspeakable union. He felt old and tired and ashamed.

'Father, what's going on? I saw Taverne riding away! You've not quarrelled with him, have you? Oh, please say you haven't quarrelled with him! I know it was wrong to try to settle matters without your leave, but one cannot help falling in love!'

Tamar had rushed in, words tumbling from her tongue.

'Sir Taverne Bostock has gone, and

will not be returning,' he said briefly.

'Gone? Gone where? Didn't he make you understand that we love each other and wish to marry?'

'There will be no marriage. I have refused my consent.'

'Refused? But why? Why have you sent him away?'

'I don't wish to discuss it,' he said coldly. 'You will have to abide by my decision.'

'Abide by — ? Father, this is my *life*!' She sprang to his side, eyes and cheeks blazing. 'This is my whole *life*, father. You cannot take the rest of my life and lock it up and throw away the key! I won't let you do that!'

'You have to trust me,' he said, not wanting to look at her but drawn by the intensity of her glance. 'You have to trust me to know what is right for you.'

'Right for me! Taverne is right for me!'

'I say not, and that should be sufficient.'

'It's not sufficient!' she said loudly.

'I'm not a child, father, and I'll not be treated like one. I love Taverne. I'll always love him. He's a fine man, from your own part of the country. There's no reason why we shouldn't be wed.'

'Save that I forbid it.'

'That's not reason enough!' she flashed. 'You have always said you'd never force me into wedlock. Now you seek to keep me from it, and you give no reason. I'll not have it so!'

'Believe me, but it gives me no pleasure to deny you,' he said.

'Denial without a reason is tyranny!'

'Mind your manners, miss,' he began, but she interrupted him furiously.

'I'll mind nothing but the truth. The truth, father! I swear that if you cannot give me your reasons for denying my marriage I'll ride after him this second and wed him without your leave!'

'Mistress! Your voice can be heard clear through to the kitchen,' Emma said hurrying in.

'He has forbidden the wedding,' Tamar said. 'He gives no reason at all, not one. He simply forbids it.'

'I'm sorry for that, sir.' Emma closed the door gently and stood between them. 'I thought the young man most charming, most eligible. I believe she would be happy with him.'

'I know I would be happy,' Tamar said. 'I shall never love any other man as long as I live.'

'She has the right to know your reasons for forbidding the marriage,' Emma said.

Her blue eyes clear, her manner firm. It was, he thought, the first time she had stepped out of her role as servant.

'The young man is unsuitable,' he said lamely, the pounding in his head increasing.

'That is no answer, sir,' Emma put. 'Forgive me for speaking so, but I want her to be happy.'

'Even if that means her marrying her own brother?' he heard himself say, and saw them as clearly as if he had never seen them before. Emma with her mouth open, Tamar with a queer, twisted smile on her lips.

Emma was the first to break the silence. In a small, careful voice she said, 'Her brother, sir?'

'When I was a boy in Cornwall I loved a girl — a wellborn lady named Catriona Bostock.'

'His mother?' Emma said.

'I went to sea after my father was drowned,' he said, weaving the tale in the most pleasing pattern his self-respect could devise. 'I hoped to make my way in the world, to make money so that I wouldn't go to her empty-handed. I came back to find her married off to a cousin of hers, another Bostock.'

'You and she — ?' Emma said.

'We were in love,' said Sir Petroc. 'Her husband was away in London, her father dead. We could not help ourselves, but there was no future for us. We agreed to part.'

It was so hard to tell the truth once the first lie had been told. And of what use to diminish himself further in his daughter's eyes by confessing he had forced the girl. As it was she was staring at him as if he were a stranger.

'I heard about the child,' he said. 'My son, whom I could never acknowledge as my own. Catriona's husband never told. The young man inherited Bostock Towers. He is proud of his lineage.'

'You are certain it is so?' Emma asked. 'That he is your son?'

'There is no possible doubt. Sir Jeremy Bostock was never a true husband to Catriona.'

'Did you tell him?' Emma whispered. 'Did you tell Sir Taverne his true identity?'

'I could not do so,' he said, and spoke the truth at last with a melancholy pride. 'I could not tell him that he has no right to the estate or the name of Bostock.'

'But he rode away,' Tamar said. She sounded lost and bewildered. 'I saw him ride away.'

'I told him it was impossible for you to wed him, or anyone, because your mother died insane.'

'You made him believe *that*?' There was real horror in her voice.

'He had no reason to disbelieve me, for he saw how much it pained me to tell it.'

'But sooner or later he will discover the truth for himself, when she weds another man,' Emma said.

'That bridge can be crossed when we reach it,' he said.

'It never will be reached,' said Tamar. 'I will never marry anyone.'

'My dear, that is nonsense!' Sir Petroc said loudly. 'You are so very young, so young that you cannot possibly say such a thing! There are many gentlemen who would be only too delighted to take you as a wife.'

'Thank you, but I'm not a doll to be handed over as a gift,' Tamar said. The colour had fled from her face and her eyes were dull. She lifted her hands in a little gesture of pleading, and then let them fall to her sides again. 'I don't blame you, father,' she said at last.

'There is no blame due to you at all.'

'Let her go, sir,' Emma said, as the door closed behind the stiff figure. 'There is nothing you or I can do now.'

'Do you blame me?' he asked.

'It's not my place,' Emma said. 'It was a long time ago, sir, when you were young.'

'Tamar is so very dear to me,' he said. 'She is the one lovely thing in my life. I'd have done anything in the world to avoid this.'

'What's done is done,' Emma said. 'We cannot turn back time, Sir Petroc.'

'She will have Ladymoon Manor, and a fortune,' he declared.

'Well, that'll be a comfort, I daresay,' Emma said, with no intention of sounding ironic. 'And she's young. That will help her too.'

'I shall take her for a holiday when the weather improves.' he said. 'New dresses, a few days' rest, some pleasant outings — ladies set store by such trifles.'

'Will you have your dinner now?' she asked.

'In half an hour. Leave me for a while. This is a — painful home-coming.'

He looked older than she had ever seen him, veins blotching the broad, reddish face, sweat trickling from beneath his wig, his hands fumbling aimlessly among the papers on the table.

'She's very young.' Emma said, 'and the young heal quickly.'

The old seldom healed, she thought, as she went out. Sir Petroc was more vulnerable than his daughter, and needed more protection.

Tamar had evidently returned to her room where she would weep bitterly no doubt. It was better that she should weep now than that Sir Petroc's whole life should crumble around him. And she, Emma Rowe, whom he had never considered as more than a servant, had the power to ruin his existence. She drew a deep breath, savouring that sense of power, holding in her mind the knowledge she had concealed for nearly twenty years.

The gaily painted caravan at the bend in the river, with the horse grazing nearby. The shabbily elegant figure glimpsed briefly once or twice. Mistress Dorothy putting on her best gown 'to go for a walk on the moors'. Her creeping back later with her shawl pulled over her head and her face glowing. And then within a few days the caravan and its occupant had gone, and the master returned from London.

'I'm with child again, Emma. Pray that this one will live.'

There had been an unspoken prayer in her eyes. 'Don't tell him about the caravan or the dark-eyed man in shabby clothes.'

'My daughter! My own precious little girl!' Sir Petroc had cried and looked with approval at his wife.

'Is she — is she like you or me?' Mistress Dorothy had asked, anxiety in her tired voice.

'Like neither of us, my sweet. She's as dark as a Romany!'

'Mistress Purity was very dark, sir, when she was younger. The child probably favours her.' Such a pretty child, showered with clothes and toys, encouraged to ride and shoot and display her temper!

'Don't curb her spirit, Emma. It amuses me to yield to her little whims. Remember she had no mother.'

And seldom a father either, for he was often away from home, building up his reputation, increasing his fortune.

'She will inherit Ladymoon Manor. 'Tis my dream to see her settled here, enjoying her rights.'

A housekeeper had no rights. She was not expected to have any passions either. She must keep house for the man she loved and bring up his child. His child! Emma's mouth curved into a melancholy smile in which the hint of power lingered.

Poor Tamar, who believed she had fallen in love with her own half-brother!

But Tamar must learn that not everything in the world was hers for the wanting. And she would have the house and the money. And Sir Petroc would never know that he had fathered an illegitimate child.

Emma wiped her hands on the white kerchief that hung from the waistband of her grey gown. Her round face had regained its serenity.

Raising her voice slightly she entered the kitchen.

'Let's not idle about all day! The master's had a long journey and needs some dinner!'

11

Tamar had never imagined that it was possible to feel so much pain for so long. It rushed upon her when she woke in the morning, darkening the day ahead, and when she lay down at night the weight of it shackled her heart.

'You must be cheerful for your father's sake. He blames himself most bitterly,' Emma said.

But it was impossible to smile, or take pleasure in anything when she knew she would never see Taverne again. That knowledge ran like a dark thread through every hour. He had ridden away believing that marriage would drive her insane.

'And I never will marry,' she said aloud. 'I could not endure to be wed to anybody else.'

They had not taken that promised

holiday after all, for the Scots were pouring over the border, gathering reinforcements as they came, sweeping south towards the capital. This rebellion was more than a flash in the pan. The Stuart prince was handsome and young, gallant as winter heather, leading the clans to what was confidently predicted would be a glorious victory.

'A Frenchified dandy with a rabble of barbarians and advisers who spend more time squabbling among themselves than talking strategy,' Sir Petroc snorted.

It was one of the rare occasions when he was at home, for most of his time was spent in York where, as one of the circuit judges, he spent days trying cases of sedition and conspiracy.

'A woman whipped through the town for speaking against the government,' Emma said, trouble in her face. 'A lad of sixteen drawn and quartered for taking two shilling so that he could run away to war.'

'I administer the law. I don't make it,' Sir Petroc said.

He had grown hard, she thought sadly. Or perhaps he had always been so and she had never known it before.

Tamar took no interest in the course of the rebellion. The house was isolated and the threat of attack a real one, but she seemed not to notice the extra bolts on the doors, nor the fact that the entire household now assembled twice a week for musket practice. She had grown quieter, her mouth drooping and her eyes dark-ringed as if sleep came reluctantly. She spent most of the day in her room, staring listlessly through the window. At table she ate greedily, stuffing herself with food as if she couldn't get enough of it, but she had grown thinner and above the fichu of her dress her collarbones were sharp and fleshless.

'You must try to forget,' Emma said. 'Good never came out of brooding over trouble.'

'Father told me once that when he

was a little boy his mother used to sing until the moon appeared in the sky.' Tamar said. 'I would sing myself a moon if I thought it would ever do any good.'

She had given the bitter little shrug with which she finished her conversations and turned again to stare through the window.

The snow had melted and rain swept the landscape, the wind battering the grass and bending the trees almost to the ground. The river was running high and the apple blossom lay thickly piled around the trunks of the trees, torn from the branches before it had fully flowered.

In the hall Sir Petroc, newly arrived from York, was taking off his cloak, handing it to the maid, raising his voice to call Emma,

'There's good news if you've a mind to hear it!' Emma was already at the foot of the stairs, hurrying through the parlour. Tamar followed more slowly, her feet dragging.

'There's been a victory at a place called Culloden,' he said. 'A complete rout for the rebels! The Pretender is in hiding, a price on his head, but he'll be caught soon, never fear!'

'That means there's no more danger then?' Emma questioned.

'None, except for the fools who followed the Stuart.' He put his arm round Tamar and kissed her. 'I can only stay for a night or two and then I must be off again to York, but I wanted you to know there is no more reason for alarm.'

'Thank heavens for that!' Emma clasped her hands in relief.

'It is the end of the Stuart pretentions,' he said in satisfaction. 'They won't try to seize the throne again in a hurry!'

He sounded pleased, Tamar thought, and a dim wonder stirred in her, that he should be pleased when men had been killed and a prince was in hiding. She moved away from him slightly, her brow furrowing, ignoring Emma's

271

quick warning glance.

'When did it happen?' she asked, politely interested.

'A week since. The news is filtering in with the despatches. The Duke of Cumberland masterminded all seemingly, more credit to him! The clans broke and fled, but the casualties were heavy. The weather was bad, but God was on the right side.'

'How fortunate for Him!' Tamar said in sudden irritation. 'Now He won't have to hide from Cumberland's men.'

'That's no way to talk,' her father said.

'I beg your pardon, father. I was just remembering that my grandfather was one of those self-same rebels,' she said.

'That was thirty years ago and has nothing to do with the present situation,' he said sharply.

'At least treason cannot be inherited,' she remarked. 'If you'll excuse me, father, I'll go back to my room.'

'You spend too much time there,' he said. 'All the pretty colour has gone from your cheeks.'

'I must remember to paint more carefully,' she said lightly.

'With the rebellion over,' Emma said brightly, 'you may be able to go out more with your father.'

'Oh, he will be too busy hanging rebels,' Tamar said.

'She talks as if she hated me,' he said when Tamar had gone.

'She's hurt by what happened and lashes out at those who are near to her,' Emma said soothingly. 'You must give her time, sir.'

'You're very patient,' he said, and gave her a tired, grateful smile.

'The rain's easing off,' the housekeeper said. 'She may take it into her head to go out later. Let her be, sir. There's time yet for her to get over it.'

'You're a good woman, Emma.' His glance was kindly. 'My aunt was right to set store by you.'

Although by nightfall the wind and the rain had ceased Tamar did not go out. She came down to supper and afterwards sat in the parlour, listening to her father and Emma discussing the events that had led to the rebel defeat.

'The Pretender might have succeeded if he had followed up his earlier successes,' Sir Petroc said. 'He is adored by the people, but he's more French than Scots. Not that it signifies, for 'tis said every good Scotsman goes to Paris when he dies!'

'Why don't you play something for us?' Emma said, glancing at Tamar. 'It's a long time since we heard a pleasant melody.'

Tamar rose docilely and went towards the spinet. The shutters had not yet been fastened and darkness was closing in around the house.

Beyond the window panes a light glinted briefly, and was gone. She narrowed her eyes, watching as the light flickered twice more and then was extinguished.

'You said you were going to play something for us,' Sir Petroc said.

There was only darkness and the

shapes of bushes in the garden now. The light had flickered three times, flickered just as she came into view behind the panes.

She sat down and began to play, gently at first and then with increasing energy. It was impossible that anyone should be able to hear beyond the walls but she played for an unseen audience, excited anticipation hastening her nimble fingers.

Shortly after nine she excused herself and went upstairs, hoping that the others would retire soon. Her father sometimes read until the small hours and Emma often sat up late by the fire. But on this evening she heard them both come up, heard Emma's respectful good-night as they parted on the landing, Sir Petroc's deeper tones and heavier step.

As a child she had lain in her bed, listening to the wind, knowing herself to be loved and protected. Now it was different, for the only love she wanted was forbidden and there was no protection against heartbreak.

The minutes dragged by. She occupied the time in changing her indoor gown for a thicker skirt and bodice.

It would be wet and muddy in the garden. She pulled on her riding boots and sat down again on the edge of her bed. Her father would take a little time to settle to sleep, and Emma, having sharp ears, might hear the drawing of the bolt.

'And I,' thought Tamar, 'am a fool. Only my intuition tells me it was Taverne who signalled me, and the most we can hope to say is goodbye.'

It was surely safe now. She opened her door cautiously, peeped out into the darkened corridor, and went cautiously downstairs. The parlour fire still glowed redly. She passed into the hall and slid back the bolts gently.

In the garden nothing stirred. The wind had dropped and only a faint drizzle blurred the view. The risen moon silvered the grass and the bushes and hedges glowed in an eerie way.

She went down the garden, her boots squelching on the muddy path and lawn. At the gate she paused, calling softly down the slope, 'Taverne! Is it you, Taverne?'

A tall figure moved out from the shadow of the trees below, and his voice came, equally soft.

'Tamar? Are you alone?'

'The others are abed. I saw the light earlier and guessed that it was you.' She was hurrying towards him, conscious of nothing but the joy of the moment.

'I prayed you would come out,' he said, grasping her hand. 'I've been skulking here all day.'

'To avoid my father?' She looked at him more closely, seeing the black stains on his sleeve. 'You're hurt!' she whispered in dismay. 'Were you attacked by footpads?'

'By Cumberland's men,' he said grimly.

'Cumberland's — ! I don't understand. Why were you fighting with Cumberland's — oh, no!' Breaking off, she stared at him.

'I rode with the Jacobites,' he said. 'I went into Scotland as a private gentleman, not caring which side accepted my services, and I met the prince.'

'And threw in your lot with him? Why? What had any of it to do with you?'

'The prince is more of a king than the one who sits on the throne,' he said tersely. 'We might have succeeded, Tamar. We might have taken the victory if he'd listened to the lairds and not to his rabble of advisers.'

'And you're hurt!'

'A sword thrust in the arm, but it won't heal properly. I lay out in the heather for three nights, listening to the screams as the wounded were bayoneted. We have walked and ridden since. We dared not enter York.'

'We?' She spoke falteringly, her eyes moving to a thinner, smaller figure emerging like a ghost from the sheltering trees.

'Maeve Mackintosh,' he said. 'She braved the sentries to find me and bring two horses she had stolen, but the poor beasts died on us.'

'You'd best come up to the house,' Tamar interrupted. 'They're all abed, so it'll be safe enough in the kitchen. Come quietly.'

She had taken his hand again, feeling his wince through her own nerves. The girl came to his other side, looking up into his face with an anxious, timid expression.

'Come,' Tamar said again.

In the big kitchen she lit candles, rekindled the fire, put water on to boil, tore linen into strips. Taverne had sunk down on the stool. Above an unshaven chin his eyes were brightly feverish, his clothes dripped water from the week's soaking. The girl stood by him, wisps of red hair escaping from her ragged shawl, her bare feet smearing blood across the rushes.

'Help him with his coat,' Tamar said impatiently. 'What use is it to stare? The wound will need to be cleansed and bound. And you'll both need something to eat.

'She's near worn out,' Taverne said.

Something in his voice made Tamar look at him sharply. There was concern in his face which approached tenderness, as the girl began to ease the coat from his shoulder.

'Who is she?' she asked. 'Why did you bring her with you?'

'I married her a month since,' he said.

'Married her?' She spoke blankly, her eyes wide.

'At Stirling,' the girl said. She had a soft, breathless little voice that lilted like birdsong. 'My father was willing for us to wed.'

'So soon?' Tamar whispered, pain slashing through her. 'You married her so soon?'

'Maeve is a good, brave soul,' he said, 'and I was sick at heart.'

'So you took consolation?' she said.

'She's a good girl,' he repeated and

there was a guilty look on his face, as if he knew very well that his marrying had constituted a kind of betrayal.

The rough dressings had stuck and the wound began to bleed afresh as she pulled them loose, but the edges of the deep slash were cleaner than she had expected.

'I packed moss into it,' Maeve said. 'Moss helps to heal.'

'Hold the basin while I see to it now,' Tamar ordered, and the girl obeyed, falling silent.

'We had nowhere else to come,' Taverne said, his voice still pleading for understanding. 'The ports are being watched for fugitives. There's a price on the head of every rebel.'

'You should have fought on the right side,' she said, briskly bandaging. 'Mistress, the broth in the cauldron is still hot. Pour out two bowls and I'll set you meat and cheese. Taverne, you'd best drink some of this madeira before you faint on me.'

She had improvised a sling, and

281

when he had drunk his colour was better. Maeve was ladling broth. She must have been less fragile than she looked or perhaps love lent her strength for the glances she bestowed upon Taverne were adoring.

'The girl had better wash her feet,' Tamar said. 'There are some boots here she can wear, and an old pair of stockings.'

'She lost her father and two brothers at Culloden,' Taverne said. 'She has nobody now except me, Tamar.'

'You're married,' she said briefly. 'Let it go at that!'

'When your father forbade me and gave me reason — '

'I said let it go,' she interrupted. 'What's done is done! You must eat quickly and then be away. The servants rise at five.'

'On foot? We need horses.'

'The stables are guarded,' she said, pulling at her lower lip with a nervous nail. 'I can get two mounts out though on the plea of exercising them. I'll bring them down to the river at first light.'

'And so help rebels to escape?' Sir Petroc's harsh question resounded from the door.

'Father! I thought you abed!' She rose in consternation as he came towards them.

'Did you so? I could not sleep, so opened the shutters and saw you crossing the garden.'

'He's wounded and in flight,' she said. 'He came to seek help.'

'From a judge who is bound to uphold the law or be taken himself for treason?'

'He came to me, father.'

'Which is worse. To shelter behind a woman's skirts, with his doxy at his side!'

'Mistress Maeve is my wife,' Taverne said.

'Aye, so I heard.' Sir Petroc's eyes swept over her contemptuously.

'She is a Mackintosh of Clan Chattan,' Taverne said.

'A Scot,' Sir Petroc said flatly. 'And

you, sir, are a selfconfessed traitor, a disgrace to your king and country!'

'You were not there,' Taverne said. 'They butchered the wounded. Some of them were locked in huts and burned alive. I saw and heard, Sir Petroc. They murdered a nation.'

'It's no time to argue politics!' Tamar cried furiously. 'They need horses, father. We can surely spare them two.'

'Help them to evade the law! You must be out of your mind,' Sir Petroc said.

He had made a gesture with his hand and two of the grooms, on command, came in.

'I roused them earlier when I came down to find the door unbolted,' Sir Petroc said. 'I too can move quietly when occasion demand. The horses are being saddled for the ride to York.'

'It's the middle of the night! You cannot mean it! Taverne, you must believe me when I tell you that he does not mean it! He will not betray you.'

'Betray? It is no betrayal to bring a

traitor to justice,' Sir Petroc said. 'I will not have them under my roof one moment longer than is absolutely necessary. We will ride to York.'

'Across the black moors on a wet night!'

'The moon is up and the rain almost ceased. We'll ride there by dawn.'

'But they will execute him,' Tamar whispered. 'They will take him out and execute him. Dear God, but you cannot do this!'

'What in the world is going on?' Emma demanded, bustling in with her robe clutched about her. 'The door is open and the men are bringing horses round! What is — ? Tamar, why are you here?'

'Taverne fought at Culloden for the Stuart,' Tamar said. 'He's been wounded and there's a price on his head.'

'And where did the girl come from?' Emma asked, staring at Maeve, who crouched, white-faced, over her bowl of cooling broth.

'She's his wife,' Sir Petroc said. 'You may well gape at the news for it's scarcely two months since he was begging for my daughter's hand. Now he is not only a traitor but has reached into the gutter to find himself a wife!'

Maeve began to cry, tears making runnels down her grimed cheeks, small sobs escaping her.

'You cannot seriously give them up to the law, sir?' Emma said, her mind whirling.

'I represent the law,' he answered her. 'I am sworn to uphold it.'

'But he's your *son!*' Tamar burst out. He's your own son!'

There was an instant silence, in the midst of which only Maeve's snuffling little sobs could be heard.

'His son?' Taverne said at last. 'What are you saying? *His* son?'

'Long ago,' Tamar said, 'when he was in Cornwall, he and your mother — they were in love.'

'So, not content with insulting my

wife, you have already slandered my mother!' Taverne said.

'It's true.' Tamar said desperately. 'That's why he wouldn't let us marry, why he spun that tale of inherited insanity. But to me he told the whole truth. He and your mother were in love and you are their child. It was kept secret to protect your mother's reputation.'

'You are my half-sister?' He spoke unbelievingly.

'We never could have married.' she said.

'My father?' Taverne's black eyes shifted to the older man. 'You are my natural father, and yet you still intend to give me up to the authorities? It's not possible.'

'You ought not to have come back here.' Sir Petroc said. 'You ought to have gone some other road. I must uphold the law.'

'You cannot have your own son executed!' Emma cried.

'Why not? He stood by and did

nothing while they beheaded his father-in-law,' Taverne said, his face black.

'I had no influence at that time,' Sir Petroc said.

'Save to persuade the daughter of Sir John Allston into wedlock,' Taverne said. 'I made enquiry at York before I rode north. A speedy wedding, the older folk recalled, and Mistress Dorothy seldom seen again. They thought it very likely that she had become feeble-minded.'

'We are talking to no purpose,' Sir Petroc said. 'The horses are saddled, I believe, and your wound has been tended. We'll leave now.'

'You really mean it, don't you?' Taverne's mouth curved downward. 'You really mean to sacrifice me to your reputation. Sir Petroc Makin, Judge, is more important than his children.'

'You ought not to have come back,' Sir Petroc repeated, the vein at his temple beating furiously. 'I cannot help you. Not now, not ever.'

He turned and went swiftly out,

riding boots ringing on the stone of the hall. The two grooms, who had stood silently by, came forward, their faces impassive.

'I'll tell them who you really are,' Tamar said. 'His reputation won't stand that scandal.'

'Neither would my mother's,' Taverne said, and put one arm about Maeve as if, in his mind, she too had become an enemy. 'I'd still be executed and her honour besmirched. Anyway, do you really imagine I care to proclaim my bastardy, or my connection with Sir Petroc? I wish to God I'd never come into Yorkshire, never met you.'

He gave a jerky little bow and walked unsteadily past her, with Maeve clinging to him.

'Emma! Emma, do something!' Tamar appealed.

'Let them alone!' Emma caught at her arm.

'But he's taking them to York, to hand them over as rebels! They'll die for treason, Emma!'

'Not until they've been tried and convicted.' The housekeeper forced calm into her voice. 'Your father may change his mind. There may be a pardon.'

'You know there won't be! He's bent on destroying him. His own son, Emma! How could he do it?'

'I'm too old to learn why men behave in the ways they do,' Emma said. 'Taverne swearing he loved you and then marrying that — girl. Who is she?'

'Maeve Mackintosh. She's not important. Emma, we have to do *something*!'

'We can clear up the mess here,' Emma said. 'Then we can have a glass of madeira and go back to bed until morning. There's nothing else to be done.'

The faint sound of galloping hooves echoed in the distance. Breaking free from Emma's restraining clasp, Tamar ran to the door. Only the rain still made fine needles in the air.

'They'll be on their way,' Emma said at her shoulder. 'Come inside now, my dear. Matters will look different in the morning.'

Tamar, closing the heavy door, thought it likely that matters would very likely look even worse.

12

'How can a man hate his son so much?'
Tamar had cried.

Emma had shrugged her shoulders
helplessly, avoiding the girl's gaze.

To Sir Petroc she might have said, 'I
know why you're doing this. In killing
your son you want to kill your own past.
I understand'.

But she could not have brought
herself to say anything. The Judge was
seldom at home these days, and when
he came he was silent and withdrawn,
saying nothing, spending long hours in
the library.

Taverne he would not discuss, but
William Marshall rode over from York
to see Tamar.

'I know you refused to wed him,' he
said, his pleasant face troubled, 'but I
guessed you'd want news.'

'You've seen him?' She kept the

292

eagerness out of her face.

'He and his wife — what an odd, silent creature she is! are lodged in the debtors' quarters. The gaol is crammed with Jacobites and more are being shipped down to Tilbury Docks to stand trial in London. I took the liberty of providing necessities for them. Food and clothing and such.'

'That was very kind of you,' Tamar said.

'Ah, well, we were at school together.' William flushed slightly. 'Friends have an obligation. His wound healed up.'

'Oh!' She drummed her fingers on the sill, looking out across the garden.

'Can't understand why he upped and turned rebel in the first place,' William said, a little disconcerted by her apparent indifference to a friend. 'A few of us did think of getting up a petition but these things never come to anything.'

'The law must take its course,' Tamar said, coolly ironic.

Inside she felt more despairing than

she had ever felt in her life.

The spring lengthened into summer and the treason trials began. Sir Petroc had gone to York and Emma, whose brother had died, had driven over to spend a few days with the widow.

'Not that I've any patience with the slattern, but when all's said and done she's kinsfolk,' Emma said. 'You'll not mind being alone?'

Tamar had shaken her head. It made no difference if she were alone or not, for she was wrapped in her own misery. Even if Taverne were not hanged he would be transported, and few of those who embarked on the fever stinking convict ships ever reached the other side.

Emma gone, and the house bathed in midday sunshine, Tamar wandered restlessly through the rooms. For the first time they gave her no sense of comfort, and when she stepped into the garden the roses mocked.

A small, plain coach rattled around the corner of the house and pulled up on the curved drive. She had been so immersed in her own thoughts that she had not been aware of its approach and she stared at it in dismay. If any of her friends had elected to call she was in no mood to receive them. In fact it had been months since she had seen any of them, and she suspected they thought her heartless for not showing any emotion at her former suitor's plight.

The coachman alighted, set down the steps, and offered his arm to the tall lady in black who descended stiffly, her lips pressed tightly together as if she were in pain and resented it.

'Mistress Makin?' The voice was imperious, the black eyes hostile.

'You are Taverne's mother.' She made the statement without surprise.

'Lady Catriona Bostock.' The woman bowed.

'Won't you come in?'

The request was acknowledged by another bow, and she led the way through to the library.

'Will you — take some refreshment?'

The tall figure leaning on an ivory headed stick intimidated her and her voice came out high and nervous.

'Not in this house,' said Lady Catriona. 'I have been staying in York and am on my way south again.'

'Then you have seen — ?'

'The trial was yesterday,' Lady Catriona said. 'An open and shut case. My son pleaded guilty and was sentenced to death, his wife to transportation for fourteen years.' She broke off, staring at Tamar's white face. 'You didn't know?' she said more gently.

Tamar shook her head.

'My son was refused leave to appeal,' Lady Catriona said. 'I was not allowed to visit him, and I was not granted an interview with the Judge. Judge! I rode a horse when he was still hauling in his father's lobster pots!'

'I tried to help Taverne,' Tamar said numbly. 'I tried to help them both to get away, but my father discovered them. Since then he has refused to discuss the matter.'

'I sat in the Court yesterday,' the other said. 'I sat and watched your father, red-robed and powerful. His face like stone. I wanted to stand up, to shout out, 'That fine upholder of English law came to my house when my husband was away and raped me! Take a long look at him, my friends, for you're unlikely to see such a hypocrite again!'

'Raped?' Tamar said. 'Raped?'

'You didn't know that either?'

'He said — a love affair, that he remained silent to protect your honour.'

'He forced me,' Lady Catriona said. 'We had been companions as young things, nothing more. But his father had been a gentleman once and Petroc had ideas above his station. He went away to sea and came back fifteen years later, expecting me still to be waiting for him. When he found out I was married he came to my home and forced me. He left Cornwall then and came up to Yorkshire. I made it my business to gather news of him from time to time. I hoped misfortune would strike him, but it never did.'

'But Taverne — his son?'

'He never even knew I'd borne a child, until I learned that Taverne wished to marry Mistress Tamar Makin, and then I went to him in London and he agreed to stop the marriage.'

'He told Taverne I was unfit for wedlock, that my mother had died insane.'

'So I gathered from a letter Taverne wrote to me. One letter and then silence, until I learned he'd married some lowborn Scot and taken up with the Jacobites.'

'He knows now that we are half-brother and sister,' Tamar said.

'And that his own father has passed sentence upon him? I ought to have stood up in that Court and screamed 'Rape'! But there's no proof of it now. They'd have called me a madwoman and locked me up. I'd not want your father to have that satisfaction.'

'What are you going to do?' Tamar asked.

'Petition the king who will not listen. King George likes to make an example of highborn gentlemen who espouse the Stuart cause. My lands have been taken from me already.'

'But you are no Jacobite!'

'In law Bostock Towers belongs to my son,' Lady Catriona said bitterly. 'It has been requisitioned by the Crown. I sold my jewels to buy passage on a vessel bound for the American Colonies. The ship sails in four days. I hoped for acquittal or pardon, but I should have learned long ago that your father has no pity.'

'And the king won't listen?'

'I have to try,' Lady Catriona said. 'I cannot rest unless I try.'

'There is another way,' Tamar said slowly. 'Escape? Others have escaped from prison.'

'The gaol is too well guarded.'

'But a letter from my father, releasing

Taverne into your custody? Might that serve?'

'Your father would never write such a letter.'

'But I can write,' Tamar said eagerly. 'I can even seal it. My father keeps a spare seal here, for when he is working on documents at home. A paper with his seal on it might fool the gaol guard.'

'Would it be possible?' The older woman's voice lifted with unexpected hope.

'It's a chance,' Tamar said. Her misery was evaporating as decision flooded to her. Anything was better than day after day of waiting for the worst in the loneliness of the quiet house.

'We can go back to York,' she said. 'We can have the horses changed and set out as soon as we've eaten.'

'We?'

'I can't stay here,' Tamar said. 'I can't stay here to face my father when he comes home again. I don't want to see him again and I don't want any part of

300

anything that belongs to him. Not Ladymoon Manor, not anything!'

'But where would you go?'

'With you.' Tamar was frantically searching for paper. 'To the Colonies with you, Lady Bostock.'

'My dear child!'

'Child? I shall never be a child again,' Tamar said bitterly. 'I love Taverne still, you see. Oh, I know he's my brother and there can never be anything between us, but love can be expressed in many ways, can't it? It isn't wrong to love, is it?'

'Not if it's legitimate love.'

'He has a wife now,' Tamar said, her mouth drawn in as if she tasted vinegar, 'and I shall never marry now. But you and Taverne have been most cruelly wronged by my father. Couldn't I set it right in some way?'

'Then give me the seal.'

'And leave me to face my father? I'll risk the Colonies,' Tamar said with a new grim humour. 'Here's the seal! My writing is something like my

301

father's, but they'll not look closely when they see the seal. I'll put that Sir Taverne Bostock and his wife are to be released on bail, pending further investigations. That sounds official, doesn't it?'

'Very official,' Lady Catriona said. For the first time a gleam of humour showed in her eyes. 'It's a pity females are not permitted to practise law! They display at least as much cunning as a Judge.'

'My father may not discover what has happened for some little while,' Tamar said, sharpening a quill. 'I'll leave word for Emma that my father has called me to York, and that will prevent her giving the alarm. You said the ship sails in four days?'

'I have passages only for three.'

'I'll bring my jewels and buy my own,' Tamar said.

'My dear, are you quite sure you really want to do this?' Lady Catriona asked. 'This is your home.'

'I don't want it and I don't want to

lay eyes on my father again,' Tamar said.

'And Taverne?'

'I shall learn to love as a sister loves,' Tamar said. 'After all, I don't have any other choice, do I?'

Within an hour they had eaten a hastily prepared meal and the horses were ready. A scribbled note left with one of the maids informed Emma that Sir Petroc had sent for his daughter to go to York.

Tamar, the carefully written document sealed, her jewels in a drawstring bag, some dresses packed in a small trunk, moved calmly and quickly. It was as if some other person, older and harder than her hurt, bewildered self, had taken over her thinking, and this person acted with unsentimental decision, her hands steady, her mind clear.

'Taverne's wife is smaller than I am. I'll take two of Emma's dresses for her. Did you bring a change of clothing for Taverne?'

'Everything he'd left at Bostock

Towers. I'd so hoped for his release.'

For the first time the proud old voice trembled. The person that was Tamar said, without pity, 'We have a very long journey ahead. Are you certain you'll not slow us down by falling ill?'

'I'll not delay you,' Lady Catriona said.

'Good. If you're ready then?' Tamar drew the hood of her travelling cloak over her black hair and went out to the waiting coach without allowing herself a single look back.

'What of the coachman?' she asked as they jolted across the moor.

'He's an old servant and completely loyal. When we've embarked he'll sell the coach and join his daughter. She's married to a Welshman and lives in some God-forsaken place up in the mountains. Mistress, are you certain you want to come? You're very young.'

'I don't want to argue about it,' Tamar said in the new, hard little voice. 'Would you have it on your conscience that you left me behind to face my father's anger?'

The other shook her head slowly.

They rattled into York as the shadows were lengthening. Tamar could not avoid remembering other occasions when she had driven into the bustling city. Emma had brought her as a child to have her fitted for new gowns, to attend sedate parties with other privileged children. But it was foolish to think of Emma, who was now part of the past from which she was struggling to escape.

'We ought to change the horses before we leave,' she said aloud, 'but it would be more prudent to wait until we reach Bradford. Can you wait for me in the street at the back of the castle?'

'You're not going into the prison alone?' Lady Catriona's voice was alarmed.

'You went there, didn't you, to ask if you could see Taverne? They may remember you. It's not likely I'll be recognised, but if I am it's scarcely likely that I would be conniving at the escape of a Jacobite! I'll be as quick as possible.'

She was already climbing down to the cobbles, her face resolute within her hood. Over her loomed the bulk of the handsome prison building erected forty years before. She had passed by often but had never entered its portals. For a moment the enormity of what she was doing made her legs shake. Then she drew a deep breath, swallowed, and went briskly up the shallow steps beneath the arch.

'Yes, mistress?' The voice that halted her was politely firm, the man tall and neatly dressed.

'You have two prisoners here,' she began.

'We have hundreds,' he said dryly. 'Which particular two do you mean?'

'They were condemned yesterday. Sir Taverne Bostock and his wife.'

'I recall them, but they are not allowed visitors. Those who've been sentenced are not allowed visitors.'

'These are to be released pending

306

further investigation. I have a letter.' She handed it to him, and stood, outwardly quiet, as he scanned it.

'It looks all right,' he said at last, 'but I don't know Sir Petroc's hand.'

'His seal is there.' She pointed to it. 'Or are you not willing to accept an official seal?'

'I'm to release them? On my own responsibility?'

'On Sir Petroc's responsibility.'

He frowned, looking from the document to her. 'And who might you be then, mistress?' he asked slowly.

'Emma Rowe, housekeeper to Sir Petroc.'

'Why would the Judge send you, and not one of the constables?' he enquired.

'I'm not in his confidence to that extent,' she said. 'I only know that he gave me this and that the two prisoners are to be set free. There's a plain coach waiting in the street. I believe the Judge wants it done quietly.'

'You mean they have agreed to turn

King's Evidence?' He lowered his voice.

'I don't know. I only know what I was told.' She waited a moment, then said, her heart racing, 'You are welcome to make enquiry from Sir Petroc if you choose, but he was in a bad humour when I left his lodging, so I'll not answer for his mood, if you question this.'

He was still doubtful, but it was evident that he knew something of her father's uncertain temper, for, after biting his lip and frowning, he nodded.

'If you wait here, mistress, I'll get two release papers. It's in order for me to keep the Judge's letter, I suppose? My superior's due in an hour, and I'd not want any trouble.'

'It's no use to me. Must I wait here? I'm not particularly fond of gaols.'

'Most folk here have the same opinion,' the guard said. 'Where's this coach you mentioned?'

'At the side gate.'

'Near the exercise yard? I can send

them out that way, I suppose. Look, you go along and wait in the coach, mistress.'

'Thank you.' She nodded in what she hoped was a briskly official manner.

It had been easy. Not until she was back in the coach did she realise that her palms were covered in sweat. Lady Catriona said nothing, but in her haggard face the black eyes burned like coals.

The minutes were like hours. A dozen possibilities raced through Tamar's mind. The guard might look more closely, not at the seal, but at the forged signature. His superior might return early and require an endorsement of the Judge's orders. Taverne might guess this was an escape and betray his relief.

The carriage door was wrenched open and Maeve, still clutching her ragged and filthy shawl, was thrust within. Behind her, Taverne, muffled in shabby cloak and low-crowned tricorn, bent his head beneath the door.

The steps were withdrawn, the door slammed. At what seemed an infuriating slow pace the horses moved off.

'You here, Tamar!' Even in the gloom of the interior she could see the confused bewilderment on his face.

'Mistress Tamar arranged the whole matter,' his mother said.

'Oh?' His glance was puzzled.

'We can explain it later, we're on our way to Liverpool, but we'll buy horses and have a meal at Bradford.'

'There's an inn just beyond the town,' Tamar remembered. 'Emma was talking about it some months since. The innkeeper's son was taken up for sedition and he was very bitter against the authorities.'

'And would likely wink at Jacobites?' Lady Catriona nodded approvingly. 'Then we'll risk spending the night there.'

'We?'

'Tamar — you will pardon my using your Christian name! — Tamar is coming with us.'

'Coming where? Am I to be told?' he demanded.

'To the Colonies,' his mother said calmly. 'You'll have a more comfortable passage than your wife would have had in the convict ship. Tamar has deceived her father and would be a fool to stay behind, for if he condemned one child he's likely to condemn another! Does that wife of yours ever open her mouth to speak? She can understand English, I take it?'

'She is half out of her wits with shock,' he excused, putting his arm around her.

'She doesn't look to me as if she was ever completely in her wits,' Lady Catriona said drily. 'You were a fool to rush into marriage with a Highland savage, my son. I only hope we shall manage to put a little polish on her when we reach a new land.'

'But what of Bostock Towers?' he asked.

'Requisitioned,' she said briefly. 'No point in crying about it. We must look

311

ahead now, not back. What is it? Why are we stopping?'

'Soldiers ahead,' Tamar said. 'They're blocking the road ahead.'

'What are we to do?' Maeve whimpered, shrinking against Taverne.

'I'll deal with this,' Lady Catriona said.

Her voice was firm, her head high. As the sound of voices grew louder, she pulled down the side window and peered out.

'Is there any trouble, sergeant? We're bound for the physician in Bradford.'

'Physician?'

'My daughter-in-law is near her time, and our private doctor is at Bradford. He is the only one who understands her case.'

'You'd better turn back to York, mistress,' the soldier said.

His face was framed briefly in the window space. Maeve uttered a little moan of terror.

'It's a difficult case. She's already

lost two babies,' Lady Catriona said, blocking his view adroitly. 'Are we to pass on, or would you and your men care to assist at a birthing?'

'We're hunting Jacobites, ma'am, not babies,' he said alarmed.

'Jacobites! You don't think they'll delay us?'

'They'll be running too fast. Do you need an escort? This is a bad road, and the light's fading.'

'All the more reason for us to be allowed to travel without hindrance!' she snapped.

'I'm sorry, ma'am. Drive on!'

The face at the window vanished and they moved on again, the horses picking up speed as the track curved downward.

'We can make Bradford by midnight, I trust?' Lady Catriona said.

'The whole scheme is — you cannot hope to travel clear across to Liverpool and embark there without being stopped,' Taverne said.

'I think we have an excellent chance,'

his mother retorted. 'We will be rested and fed and have changed our clothes when we leave the inn. A family party, travelling home, should excite no suspicion.'

'Save that I am wanted for treason, and by harbouring me you bring great danger upon yourselves. Tamar will be missed very soon.'

'Emma is staying with her sister-in-law,' Tamar said. 'I left word that I'd been called to my father in York. And for yourself, with so many prisoners coming and going, it's likely that nobody will check on your release for several days.'

'Provided that Scot you wed keeps as quiet as she is now, we should do well,' Lady Catriona finished.

Maeve's breathless lilt sounded in the gloom, 'I'd not bring danger to you. If you like you can set me down here and drive on.'

'The girl is most certainly half-witted!' Lady Catriona said. 'If she were apprehended there would certainly be questions asked about the rest of us. I've no desire to arrive in the Colonies on a convict ship, leaving my son dangling at the end of a rope! The idea of leaving her here!'

She sounded, thought Tamar, very slightly ashamed of herself.

It was growing darker but the calm weather was holding. The coachman paused briefly to set flares at each side of his seat, and then they were off again over the wide track, bouncing in the deep ruts.

At every jerk Lady Catriona's face grew whiter and once she made an audible gasp of pain which she turned into a cough. Opposite Maeve slept fitfully, her head on Taverne's shoulder. Taverne himself had fallen silent, his eyes brooding. It was becoming too dark to see clearly but Tamar sensed he was watching her.

A feeling of unreality stole over her. She ought to be asleep in her own bed, not fleeing across country with these strangers. For a moment fear shivered through her, and then Lady Catriona patted her arm in a quick, shy gesture of friendship and Maeve whimpered in her sleep like a child needing protection.

Epilogue

The ship rode the waves like a bird, its sails winging wide above their heads. The weather had remained fair, though the Captain had warned of squalls ahead.

'Fortunately,' said Lady Catriona, 'I've always been an excellent sailor. You too seem to have adapted very swiftly to life aboard, my dear.'

She gave Tamar an approving glance and sniffed slightly as Maeve and Taverne came into view. The Scots girl was as small and thin as a child, and her recent seasickness had made her seem even more fragile, dulling her red hair and whitening her already pale cheeks.

Taverne was settling her into a seat, wrapping a blanket more closely around her. He had devoted himself to his silent, ailing wife ever since they had set sail, carrying tiny portions of food in the hope of tempting her to eat a morsel, patiently enduring her weeping when the vessel rolled for Maeve was certain they would all sink to the bottom the moment the wind blew.

Now he sat next to her, chafing her hands and talking in a low, encouraging voice. Tamar looked away, out across the rippling water.

'You still love him, don't you?' Lady Catriona had lowered her own voice and her sharp eyes were kind.

'I am learning to think of him as my brother,' Tamar said stiffly.

'But it's not easy, eh? To have to watch him falling in love with his wife day by day? He wed her on impulse, my dear, forgetting the duty he owed to his station in life, but the girl needs him. She's fragile and needs to be cherished and guided, but she loves him and is grateful to him, and that is a most flattering inducement to a man!'

'I shall manage,' Tamar said.

'I've no doubt you will,' Lady

Catriona agreed. 'You're one of the strong ones of the earth, my dear. You'll bend, not break, unless the winds twist you. Then I'd not answer for the consequences.'

'I was thinking of Ladymoon Manor,' Tamar said. 'Of my father and Emma, and what they'll say when they find me gone. By now they'll surely know.'

'Do you regret it?' the other said.

Tamar was silent, while there rose in her mind a picture of the stone house, its many chimneys puffing smoke, wind stirring the ivied mullions and scattering petals from the blossoms in the orchard.

'A new land,' said Lady Catriona. 'We have no connections there and very little money. This passage is costing us three times the usual. And we have little hope of ever being able to return, for I cannot imagine amnesty being granted to the Jacobites. Even if they did, could you bear to live again with the Judge?'

'I hate him,' Tamar said.

'Hold to that,' Lady Catriona advised. 'Hate is a great source of strength if you keep it smouldering, unmixed with regret or pity. I have hated your father for more than thirty years. It has given me great strength.'

'We'll make a good life in the Colonies,' Tamar said, banishing from her mind the picture of Ladymoon Manor. 'It will be a new beginning.'

'And your love for Taverne?'

'As a sister for her brother,' said Tamar and looked out resolutely across the water.

At Ladymoon Manor the servants went about their work in an unaccustomed silence. Forbidden to talk about the one subject that interested them on pain of instant dismissal, even possible arrest for sedition, they kept their own counsel within doors, waiting for the moment when, their duties over and the Judge retired for the night, they could whisper round the kitchen fire.

'Mistress Tamar helped a Jacobite to escape from York.'

'And the Jacobite her own brother! A by blow of Sir Petroc's from his young days in Cornwall.'

'But they wished to marry. This is against the law, isn't it?'

'Of course it's against the law. Sir Taverne wed another lady.'

'A Jacobite, not a lady!'

'Well, another female anyway. It means Mistress Tamar cannot wed him twice over.'

'But Sir Petroc sentenced him to death.'

'For being a traitor, not for trying to marry Mistress Tamar!'

'His own son.'

'Bastard — there's a difference.'

'It's still kinfolk. Sir Petroc is a hard man.'

'They look at me as if I were a monster,' Sir Petroc said. He was in the library, a half empty decanter of brandy at his side. Under his curled white wig his face was puffy, for lack of sleep.

Emma, hair neatly coiled, was seated on a lower chair, her hands occupied with a piece of knitting.

'You ought not to mind them,' she said placidly. ' 'Tis a nine days' wonder, that's all.'

'I've offered more money,' he said. 'Ten thousand guineas for information leading to Tamar's apprehension. So far thirty people claim to have seen her.'

'The sergeant who stopped the coach outside York?'

'It sounded promising, but the trail went cold at Bradford. That damned innkeeper knew something, but he wasn't talking, and neither were his servants. I sent runners into Cornwall but nobody has seen them there either.

'They'll have sailed away by now. She took her jewels.'

'Left England? She'd never do that. Ladymoon Manor is her home. She loves the place as much as I do. She'd never leave it.' He gulped his brandy and said loudly, 'Must you knit? There is nothing more provoking than a woman with restless hands.'

'I beg your pardon, sir.' She folded

her work away neatly into its bag.

'She's all I have,' he said. 'The one person I've ever really loved without selfishness. My parents — it's no virtue to love one's parents. And I'll admit but there were times when I was ashamed of them. My father was a gentleman but he seemed not to care. He was happy, scraping a living from the farm and the sea. He loved my mother very much, you see, but she limped and she had lost her beauty, save when she sang the moon. She was beautiful then.'

'Lady Catriona?' she ventured.

'She was rich and lovely, with a home like the home I'd dreamed about,' he said. 'Her father despised me, and sent me away, but I went on loving the thought of her. Fifteen years at sea, Emma. Fifteen years and most of it hell. And then coming back, to find my mother dead and the farm gone, and Catriona still despising me.'

'But you said — '

'That we were in love. It wasn't so,' he said heavily. 'I forced her to it,

Emma. I took her and used her and rode north to meet my father's sister.'

'You loved her,' Emma said.

'Because she owned Ladymoon Manor,' he said bluntly. 'I wanted it, you see. I wanted to own it, and to marry and to bring up my children here.'

'Mistress Dorothy.'

'Was my means to an end. For a long time I thought she would never bear a living babe. And then Tamar was born. I adored my daughter, Emma. It has been for her sake that I've worked to increase my fortunes, to better my reputation.'

It was, she knew, only partly true. He had worked in the dimly acknowledged hope that Lady Catriona would regret her refusal of him. But he had forgotten that motive, and believed now that he had done everything for the sake of his daughter.

'Tamar would never leave England,' he repeated. 'She has behaved badly, very badly, but she is young and headstrong. Spoiled, I fear. You and I have spoiled her a little, Emma, but she's a good girl. At heart she's a good girl.'

'What will you do sir, if — when she returns?' the housekeeper said.

'Welcome her!' he returned promptly. 'Welcome her home with open arms. No recriminations of any kind, I promise you. Fortunately the guard who accepted that ridiculous document is too terrified of the possible consequences to his own position to say anything. I believe the affair can be glossed over as a mistake, an unfortunate clerical error.'

'But you sentenced him!' Emma exclaimed. 'You were ready to see him hang.'

Sir Petroc leaned to pour more brandy, splashing it over the edge of his goblet as his hand shook violently.

'I had to do my duty,' he said. 'I must administer the law which I swore to uphold when I accepted the position of Judge. Personal feelings don't enter into the matter.'

But that was not true, he thought. When he looked at Taverne he saw himself at the same age violent and bitter. He saw himself tearing at Lady Catriona's gown, pulling the flowered ribbons from her long black ringlets, saw her on the floor, skirts rumpled, eyes cold as stones. He had hated himself, he realised, for many years. In sentencing Taverne to death he had sought to kill that part of himself that had acted without honour or compassion.

'Tamar will come home,' he said loudly, as if daring anybody to contradict him. 'She will come home again, I tell you.'

'Yes, sir.' Emma rose and stood, waiting respectfully. 'You'll keep her room ready for her,' he ordered. 'You'll keep her remaining dresses washed and ironed, the spinet tuned, her place laid at table. And bring me another bottle of brandy! This one is badly decanted!'

'Won't you have something to eat, sir?' she questioned. 'There's a tasty roast duckling.'

'Later. I'll have something later,' he said impatiently. 'Send someone with the brandy in a few minutes.'

'Yes, sir.' She bobbed a curtsy, but he was staring down into his goblet and never answered.

She went through to the kitchen and relayed the order, frowning when Cook remarked that it was the third bottle decanted in two days.

The manor house was quiet. There were no bits of abandoned frippery tossed over the chairs, no young voice calling impatiently for her horse to be saddled, no quick gliding footsteps to disturb the silence.

Tamar was gone. The child she had loved and reared and resented was gone, and Sir Petroc would wait for her return.

Emma opened the door into the little-used prayer-room and bolted it behind her. The room was sunlit, rays of gold slanting through the high round window to the carpet and panelled walls and a few pieces of heavily carved furniture. She was the only one who ever came here and sometimes she had the quaint idea that the little room was lonely.

Bending she pulled back the carpet and slid aside the tile. The cup was a warm, living thing between her hands. She sat back on her heels and stared at the carved silver face. The woman's great, slanting eyes gazed back at her, neither blaming nor approving.

'She has to return,' Emma whispered, 'for if she does not you may lie hidden for a hundred years. But until she comes back I am mistress here, as I always dreamed.'

The face stared impassively, the cup growing heavier. The room was growing larger, opening out, becoming a place she had never seen. There was a faint perfume in the air and the ringing of bells.

Priests in leopard skins and girls with golden serpents on their brows circled in slow procession. She saw them clearly, perfume cones on their hair, lotus blossoms round their wrists. And holding the cup two hands, workworn and tired. The hands grew old, flesh shredding from green bones, and then a child laughed somewhere and the hands were young and pink again, the perfume stronger, the chanting louder.

It was cold even though the sun still beat into the little room, and against the delicate carving her hands looked ugly, the flesh coarse, red-veined, the nails curved greedily.

'He ought to have married me,' Emma said. 'I would not have betrayed him with a passing stranger, nor rejected him, nor given him pain. Tamar ought to have been my child, and this house mine. His aunt was always fond of me. She showed me this cup, gave me the power of revealing the secret of its existence or not as I chose. Well, I'll not tell him. I'll wait until Tamar comes home.'

She bent forward, replacing it carefully, her plump face serene.

On the moonlit deck Taverne spoke in a rapid undertone without looking at his companion.

'I will always love you, Tamar, but such love is forbidden, so I'll not speak of it again, nor seek occasion to be alone with you. I'll cherish little Maeve and help us build a new life together free from the past and its hatreds. We'll be comrades, Tamar, but not lovers. Never lovers, except sometimes in our minds when the moon is high. But the moon stays up in the sky and we cannot call it down to satisfy our heart's yearnings.'

He went from her before she could answer, cautious on the sloping deck. Tamar gripped the rail and raised her face to the bright crescent of silver. A song of the Cornish grandmother she had never seen, hummed in her childhood by her father came into her head. A sweetly haunting song it had been to draw the soul from the breast and the moon down the sky, but she could not remember the right tune to sing.

Other titles in the
Linford Romance Library:

CONVALESCENT HEART

Lynne Collins

They called Romily the Snow Queen, but once she had been all fire and passion, kindled into loving by a man's kiss and sure it would last a lifetime. She still believed it would, for her. It had lasted only a few months for the man who had stormed into her heart. After Greg, how could she trust any man again? So was it likely that surgeon Jake Conway could pierce the icy armour that the lovely ward sister had wrapped about her emotions?

TOO MANY LOVES

Juliet Gray

Justin Caldwell, a famous personality of stage and screen, was blessed with good looks and charm that few women could resist. Stacy was a newcomer to England and she was not impressed by the handsome stranger; she thought him arrogant, ill-mannered and detestable. By the time that Justin desired to begin again on a new footing it was much too late to redeem himself in her eyes, for there had been too many loves in his life.

MYSTERY AT MELBECK

Gillian Kaye

Meg Bowering goes to Melbeck House in the Yorkshire Dales to nurse the rich, elderly Mrs Peacock. She likes her patient and is immediately attracted to Mrs Peacock's nephew and heir, Geoffrey, who farms nearby. But Geoffrey is a gambling man and Meg could never have foreseen the dreadful chain of events which follow. Throughout her ordeal, she is helped by the local vicar, Andrew Sheratt, and she soon discovers where her heart really lies.

HEART UNDER SIEGE

Joy St Clair

Gemma had no interest in men — which was how she had acquired the job of companion/secretary to Mrs Prescott in Kentucky. The old lady had stipulated that she wanted someone who would not want to rush off and get married. But why was the infuriating Shade Lambert so sceptical about it? Gemma was determined to prove to him that she meant what she said about remaining single — but all she proved was that she was far from immune to his devastating attraction!

HOME IS WHERE THE HEART IS

Mavis Thomas

Venetia had loved her husband dearly. Now she and their small daughter were living alone in a beautiful, empty home. Seeking fresh horizons in a Northern seaside town, Venetia finds deep interest in work with a Day Centre for the Elderly — and two very different men. If ever she could rediscover love, would Terry bring it with his caring, healing laughter? Or would it be Jay, the once well-known singer now at the final crossroads of his troubled career?

THE ELUSIVE DOCTOR

Claire Vernon

Wearing spectacles to make herself appear more dignified, twenty-year-old Candy gained the longed-for post as secretary to the two principals of a school in the African mountains. She was often overworked, sometimes shocked, occasionally unhappy. But all through her days at the school there ran a single thread, which bound her to the one person with whom she felt most at ease, the man who finally said unforgivable, hurtful things — the man she could not forget.